Travel among Men

Travel among Men

stories by
Kathleen Lee

Center for Literary Publishing
and University Press of Colorado
Fort Collins, Colorado

Copublished by the Center for Literary Publishing
and the University Press of Colorado.
Set in Sabon and Braganza.
Printed in the United States of America by Maple-Vail.
Jacket designed by Nicole Hayward and printed by Pinnacle Press.

The author gratefully acknowledges the publications in which the
following stories previously appeared: "Travel among Men,"
Colorado Review; and "Norris" (as "Still Life"), *Puerto del Sol.*

Library of Congress Cataloging-in-Publication Data

Lee, Kathleen.
Travel among men : stories / by Kathleen Lee.
p. cm.
ISBN 1-885635-03-6 (hardcover : alk. paper)
1. Voyages and travels—Fiction. 2. Travel—Fiction. I. Title.
PS3612.E344 T73 2002
813'.6—dc21
2001006842

1 2 3 4 5 06 05 04 03 02

This book is for people I have met traveling

Contents

Acknowledgments

For their assistance with details, critical reading, and good advice; for friendship; and sometimes for a combination of all of these things, I thank Sheila Black, Robert Boswell, Mary Feidt, Sarah Hamilton, Laura Hendrie, Tony Hoagland, Gerald & Darlene Lee, Eddie Lewis, Ben Livant, Richard McCann, Kevin McIlvoy, Christina Montes de Oca, Toni Nelson, Luann Overmyer, Alex Parsons, Jack Parsons, Miriam Sagan, Henry Shukman, and Pamela Weisse. I'd also like to thank Stephanie G'Schwind and David Milofsky.

Travel among Men

Travel among Men

"To whom do you belong?"

Breathy, sibilant delivery. Pathetic as a pick-up line. Most words men slipped into her ears carried the ballast of seduction. What did he mean? Country? Family? Never look a Muslim man in the eyes. If you answer even the most innocent of questions, you may be followed for days. A yes or no, the phrase "the United States" will spur the questioner into a determined pursuit.

Lili was going to a place rumored to be Shangri-La along the Pakistan-Afghanistan border. Her hair was dirty, she hadn't had a shower or bath in nine weeks, her stomach struggled to accommodate a variety of microscopic inhabitants, and there were scabs on her scalp where no injury had occurred. She counted. She'd been traveling for ten and a half months, she'd had intestinal parasites for three months, she hadn't spoken to anyone who knew her well for four months. She had spent one hundred and two days in Muslim territory. This was her one hundred and twenty-seventh pre-dawn departure, and she had awakened to find her second scorpion on the floor beside the bed she'd slept in. Nobody knew where she was. No one—she belonged to no one. The empty, exhilarating echo of this inside her.

She ignored her questioner, striding through the frozen, lumpy mud of the street. Night was almost at end, the sky a flat black, the stars dim, a slim moon bent above the tops of the stone buildings. The snowy peaks at the end of the valley were stainless steel shadows. There was the pungent smell of mud and the knife edge of cold in her nose. The temperature seemed to have dropped, the way it often did just before dawn.

At the bottom of the street she waited with a group of men for jeeps, already packed with supplies, to fill with passengers. Waiting was inevitable. She waited for food to be served, for vehicles to arrive or depart, for the weather to change, for her fate. Now she waited for Jerard, a chatty Frenchman. He was full of sarcasm and slightly believable stories. Jerard knew someone in Krakel, he had told her, the last village before the border with Afghanistan, so he was coming along on this journey. God, what had gotten into her? Where had her principles gone? Like a mouth sore, she kept touching the previous night's events. Nothing wrong with a little random sex, but what a poor choice: he was old, greedy, apt to attach himself to her.

The men, several with rifles and the twined white turbans of Pathans, pivoted on their heels in order to watch Lili. She turned her back. Even though her hair was covered and her figure shadowy beneath loose clothes, even though she was not beautiful, Lili was a woman and alone, an enflaming combination. How tedious.

The sky turned light enough to watch an airborne chase between four fighter jets. The men murmured, shifted, smoked, their eyes on the sky. A bumper sticker on one of the jeeps read, "Trust the Soviets? Ask the Afghans." It was 1987 and they were fifty kilometers from the border with Afghanistan, a full-scale war, a land mined, hungry country.

Lili traveled to borders. There was no logic to this, just her inexplicable satisfaction at standing on one piece of land gazing at another with a different name. It was a shape she imposed on a shapeless journey. She didn't really know what she was doing wandering around the world without a purpose while everyone else her age was getting married, having children, and building careers as lawyers and consultants and teachers. She was escaping an assortment of mildly dull but not terrible things in her life. She was escaping the shapelessness of her own future. She had found herself deeply pleased by the soothing sensation of moving over land; days and nights of travel on buses, vans, trains, boats. It was movement for its own sake, the goal was a fiction. The road they would take to Krakel ended in the mountains, beyond which lay Afghanistan.

One jeep filled and left. She watched Jerard approach with a man she didn't recognize. For a moment, she was glad someone else was coming. She resented the ghost of coupling that haunted her travels with men. She leaned away as Jerard bent to kiss her cheeks. He looked her over, eyes moving slowly up the length of her body. *"Mais qui est jolie ce matin?"* he laughed. Who looks lovely this morning? "Sorry I'm late—I slept terribly last night." He paused to wink meaningfully at her. "Couldn't get out of bed. Too much coffee, not enough drugs." He was fiddling with his Pakistani cloak and cap—casting charming little smiles at Lili—then stuffing his bag into the back of the jeep between the sacks of lentils, ammunition crates, and a raw slab of goat meat with strips of white fat like lines of snow. The goat head, eyes staring into the sky, and the four severed ankles and hooves, were tucked into a corner.

She forced herself to look at him directly. He was tall and thick-featured, with straggly ink-black hair, a beard, and heavily lidded pale blue eyes. He looked permanently hungover, an impressive feat in a dry country. She didn't know him at all; she knew him in ways she regretted. The images that flickered through her brain brought a wave of nauseating anxiety: the hair in a spout from his groin to his belly button, his hips between her thighs, his pillowy lips. Her brain went blank; no penis images allowed—it was enough that she was surrounded by them, even if they were hidden from view. She didn't want a man, the same man, around.

"Lili, this is Gustavo. I found him in the Mountain Home last night. He's from Guatemala," he said.

Gustavo greeted Lili, looking at her too long, too intently. She hated these meaningful glances. A brief sensation of panic, a thrill of regret filled her.

"His English is very good, you'll see. He wants to go to Shangri-La. He thinks it's going to cure him of his troubles." Jerard shrugged. "I explained that it's more a place in your mind than in the world."

"I want to see it," Gustavo said.

"There's nothing to see." Jerard hacked and spat. "Shangri-La is the land of happy-ever-after, but that's nothing to touch or see, eh?" He took out a plastic bag and small spoon and began spooning a white powder into his mouth. "It's sugar," he explained. "It calms me." Sugar? Jerard had been in Berkeley in the sixties, still owned a farm in Bolivia and a house in Kabul full of millions in art and rugs, plus a pet monkey that he'd had to abandon when the Russians invaded. He was living in Chitral, the town they were leaving, but it was November and getting colder, so he was considering a move to the beach in India. He appeared unconcerned about money or meaningful activities.

She felt suddenly weary; she didn't want to go into the mountains of Pakistan with two men. She pictured herself singular; the pristine quality of the days, buried in the dense silences of a foreign language; a world of gestures and facial expressions, human interactions falling into the soft vagueness of sepia-toned photographs with blurred edges and a romantic hazy light. A world absent of men gaping at her. But, with or without these two particular men, men would gape.

Jerard, Lili, and Gustavo squeezed onto the vacant bench seat in the back. The driver, Wazir, cranked the engine; his brother, Mohammed, took the front passenger seat, and the jeep lurched over a mangled, narrow road, past mud houses, grazing goats, and children standing in doorways, raw faced and unwashed. Wazir stopped and all the men got out to urinate; the Pakistanis squatting and fumbling beneath their baggy *shalwar-kameez*, the other two with their backs to Lili and the wind, sending arcs down toward the Mastuj River. They were on a ridge of boulders above a wide flood plain without a tree or substantial rock for miles, nothing Lili considered adequate cover from the vigilant gazes of four men. The Hindu Kush rose before them, worn, heavy-bottomed mountains furry with pines. Female mountains; a feminine landscape dominated by men. She waited.

Her parents' idea of travel was driving from Pasadena

to rural Illinois to visit relatives, camping out along the way, staying in a hotel every third night "to clean up." They were appalled by this trip of hers, its length as much as where it had taken her. They believed that Pasadena was the only safe place in the world because nothing had ever happened to them there. To Lili, it didn't make sense to be afraid in Pakistan but not in California; danger and disaster lurked equally everywhere and waited for her in no particular place. She *was* afraid, of familiar pain and suffering: bee stings, illness, love. And she was cavalier about the unknown: car accidents, tooth decay, foreign countries. One of her friends claimed that Lili's lack of a sufficiently vivid imagination provided her with a handicapped view of possible dangers. Lili preferred to think of herself as willfully unimaginative; some people kept themselves young, she kept herself fearless. The trick was to reside deeply in the unknown since she flinched only in the face of the known.

While Wazir drove like an out-of-control teenager, Gustavo delivered a nervous stream of chatter into Lili's ear, his words sometimes split and thrown by the wind. He didn't like Pakistan. He had come by accident, something about his girlfriend—Lili didn't catch exactly what. The food was horrific, and he hated the music, which was whining and high-pitched, like the moans of the dead. There were no women. Of what use was a country that hid its women? Gustavo was small, with child-sized feet and hands. He had skin the color of teak and round, black eyes like seeds. His expression was morose and stunned, as if he'd been ambushed by sadness. Wazir took a blind corner at full speed, rolling the slab of goat meat into Jerard's lap.

"Shit!" Jerard yelled—but it sounded like "sheet"—and pounded on Wazir's shoulder. Mohammed delicately removed tobacco from a K2 cigarette and replaced it with hash, heedless of the rough ride, the frigid wind. Jerard jammed the slab of goat behind the generator, then swiped his bloodied hands down a sack of flour, leaving streaks of red like a child's finger painting. "Pakis can't drive. It's the war next door. They're jittery and high all the time. Makes for some bad trips, man." Lili felt the faint vibration of his lips against her ear. Her proximity to him spawned a bout of self-loathing. How could she have done this to herself? Six thighs packed against each other like chicken legs on a tray. She could smell Jerard's tobacco breath, see his lips sucking at the cigarette. She imagined her life depended on this—a gun to her head; she must sit calmly between these two men.

Wazir yanked the jeep to a halt, and he and Mohammed sprinted down to the river. A man ran along the riverbank, throwing stones at a duck riding the current. Wazir and Mohammed took up the chase while the man ran to retrieve a rifle from the rocks. The duck rose and fell in the choppy, silted waters of the river, unaware of the craving it had created.

Lili, Jerard, and Gustavo watched from the road. Jerard lit another cigarette. "Fools. It will only drown if they shoot it."

"Hunger," Gustavo said.

"Protein," Lili added.

"Bullshit," Jerard said. "Wazir and Mohammed own this jeep, eat as much mutton as they want. I ate a huge hunk of meat with them last night. They aren't hungry."

The wind pummeled the shouts of the men into spare, meager sounds. The shots of the rifle, too, were whipped away into something weedy and insignificant. The three men waved their arms at each other in incomprehensible signals. Peaks loomed above the river, shadowing the scene.

Sunlight lay between the shadows like the shapes of God spread across rock and water. The men flapped, desirous and timid, at the edges of those big-hipped mountains. Lili imagined she was in a foreign film, black and white scenes without dialogue, with Stravinsky or Philip Glass and Ravi Shankar in the background.

"The lure of unfamiliar flesh," Jerard said.

"Desire is not the same as need—they just look the same," Lili said.

"Exactly. I'm not talking about gastronomy," Jerard said.

"Oh, please." Lili rolled her eyes. Desire and need were about indulgence; some people indulged themselves and some didn't.

"In certain languages, the verbs *to hunt* and *to love* are the same words, you know." Jerard sucked at his cigarette, raised an eyebrow at Lili, put out a hand and pinched her cheek.

She turned her head. How to avoid anything further with Jerard without offending him. She concentrated on Wazir and Mohammed as they trudged up the hill, defeated yet satisfied. It was not, after all, the duck they cared about, but the pursuit.

In the village of Ayun, Wazir and Mohammed emptied the jeep of everything except the ammunition, and then collected passengers for the ride up the valley. Wazir was gregarious and comical, fond of slapping Jerard on the back and leering at Lili. He wore a garish, striped vest over the tunic of his *shalwar-kameez*. Mohammed was quiet, perpetually stoned, never looking at anyone directly.

Lili bought dates and apricot-pit nuts from a man sitting behind his burlap sacks, patiently doing nothing. He sat Buddha-like, a glass of tea cooling at his feet, and gazed across the flat of dirt edged with crumbling adobe buildings and rotting wooden doors. Snot-nosed children ruled the plaza. The single toy was a small, rusted tricycle that lay on its side next to three empty oil drums. Men sat in the dark of a dirt-floored teahouse; there were no women.

"You like traveling alone, being solitude?" Gustavo's mix of sometimes strange, sometimes flawless English amused her.

"Yes." The hours she'd spent playing solitaire with the deck of cards in her backpack.

He looked at the ground, rotating a booted toe in the dirt, the movement of a child. Lili wondered if, bottled, this dirt would be indistinguishable from the dirt of Mexico, of a New York City park, of mountains in the Philippines. If a scientist analyzed it, could it only be the dirt of Pakistan and no other place on earth? Gustavo covered his face with his hands, and Lili realized he was suffering. She didn't touch him; the casual or friendly gesture was gone from her repertoire. Men responded with a clammy enthusiasm that was like raw meat down her throat.

His face crumpled. "I'm sorrowed. My girlfriend went back to Switzerland."

"I thought you were ill and we'd have to go to Peshawar in a rusty van," she said. "You too sick to move, me fighting off the lecherous advances of the driver, Jerard talking too much to notice, and then, of course, the van would break down in a snowstorm."

He laughed, covering his mouth like women in Japan.

"I don't like to be alone." His style of looking directly into her eyes inspired distrust.

A boy delivered two glasses of tea on a bent metal tray. Holding the rims of the hot glasses, they sat on a couple of tires in the dirt. It was sunny and cold, with thin clouds hanging like sheets frozen on a line.

"Go to Switzerland," Lili said. What was the deal with men, anyway? Every man she met had a girlfriend. Men liked to be attached to someone somewhere, even if they were angling for other attachments someplace else.

"We had trouble in China. Now she is there and I am here." He paused to shake his head and move some dirt. "It's a terrible place, this country, terrible."

Lili didn't say anything. Pakistan seemed, like nearly every country she'd been in, both terrible and fabulous. She could no longer judge countries with the slice of a knife, good from bad.

"Do you have a husband or boyfriend?" Gustavo said.

Over and over again: variations on a routine. Endless questions about her availability, slippery attempts to determine the likelihood of getting her to take off her clothes prone on a bed somewhere. Her occasional lies about a boyfriend or husband never affected the fanfare of seduction. Maybe she had been traveling alone for too long, had encountered too many men with a single, obsessive preoccupation.

"No," she said.

"Have you been in love before?" he asked.

"Yes," she sighed. Just give in: mating was always on the conversational agenda.

"What happened?"

Men and love; anchovies and graham crackers; items that could technically be combined but at the risk of indigestion. The plaza children began throwing rocks into the eyeless sockets of the front half of a jeep left on the rooftop opposite. It was a competition. The big boys against the little boys. They flung their bodies into the air and hurled stones, pinging against the metal. Gustavo waited for her answer; maybe he really wanted to hear what she had to say. She yawned. She imagined his kind of love slithered toward a woman on its belly, wriggling enticingly. It wouldn't work with her; even if someone bashed her over the head from behind, it might not work. She had cultivated an impermeable surface. But, that slip with Jerard.

"Oh, some familiar version of the same old story. Love always seems like a new country, and then you realize you've been there already." She considered the three men she'd fallen in love with, like combination plates: Number One, Brilliance and Criticism; Number Two, Sensuality and Indifference; Number Three, Creativity and Ambivalence. These paired qualities were the traces they left like the smell of exhaust as they disappeared. She looked over at the jeep, feeling restless, ready to move.

"I love my girlfriend. Maybe." He looked into Lili's eyes, a direct gaze heavy with intention.

Well, bully for you, she thought. What was going on? Responding to men required so much effort: measuring her level of engagement, gestures, and words; considering what she meant, what they meant, what they might think she meant.

"But, I don't trust her." He shrugged elaborately. "I don't like to be alone," he said again.

The stone-throwing game ended, and two of the boys crept into the jeep. They crouched low, but a man came over, knuckled their heads, slammed the jeep door, and sent them scurrying across the plaza. Lili doubted his girlfriend trusted Gustavo either.

"Maybe you have a girlfriend?" he asked.

"No."

"Well," he laughed, "it is possible." He looked uneasy.

"Yes." She wasn't attracted to women sexually, which

left her with men and her own small-minded dissatisfactions. A friend, in the midst of some unpleasantness with a lover, had once said, "What we need is a third gender." But gender didn't eliminate problems, it multiplied them.

"*Vamanos!*" Jerard yelled from in front of the teahouse. They crammed into the jeep with ten new passengers, all men, jockeying and scuffling to sit beside Lili. Under these conditions, Gustavo and Jerard became assets. She waited until there was a lull, then squeezed between them, the air tense with longing. She didn't want anyone in this jeep to touch her; how could they want her? She wanted to detach her soul from the messy wake her female parts created. Wazir took off, two men to his right and one man on his left, the back sagging. The men whooped around corners, each grasping a piece of the jeep. The road narrowed and grew more precipitous, with long, sheer drops to a faint froth of river below. After about twenty minutes, Wazir stopped and everyone unloaded to examine two thin planks bridging a deep chasm. They lit hash cigarettes and discussed strategies for crossing. The dry, weathered planks spanned the sharpness of open air, a crashing bed of rock, and the thin, distant river. Gustavo stood back, refusing to look at the crossing or the drop. Jerard spooned sugar into his mouth. Then he inhaled on a cigarette until his cheeks collapsed inward. "Son of a bitch." Turning to Lili, he said, "What if you fell down that, out here?" He swept his arm in a wide arc.

For a minute she pictured herself twisted and broken on the rocks below. Lili shook her head. "I won't," she said with conviction.

"What are you, some kind of clairvoyant?"

"I guess I could fall. It doesn't feel like it though."

"What do you mean, *feel?* Think of it: you're going to die in twenty minutes. You know how that feels?"

She looked down into the dangerous air. "I was talking

about intuition. I don't know how it would feel to die. I think about dying, about what I'd regret. But it's disappointing because all I can think of are small things, how I'd be sad I never went over the Khyber Pass, or that I hadn't eaten a good salad recently, or hadn't taken a long, hot bath." How mediocre; the threat of death should be an incentive for action, for living a life. It shouldn't be about trivial stuff. "I'd rather die than be maimed," she added.

"No. Everyone would rather live badly than not live at all." He coughed in wrenching, muddy wheezes, cleared his throat, and spat off the cliff. Stubbing his cigarette on a rock, he watched his spit fall, then turned to Lili, stroked her cheek, bent and kissed her. The smoothness of his palm, the sweet-acrid taste of sugar and tobacco, soft lips against her own; a kiss was so many things.

Lili drew back. "What movie are you living in?" She felt wary; Jerard knew how to kiss.

"A man and woman, strangers, at the edge of a cliff, about to risk their iives to cross it for the sake of risk itself, turn to each other and kiss. The wind behind them, the sky darkening with clouds. What about romance?" He saw her skepticism. "What's wrong with you? Women are never content with what they can have—they always want more. They must have, like a possession, a man's soul." Jerard lit another cigarette, holding his face away from Lili, but she saw his hands shaking.

"I don't want your soul, Jerard," Lili said. And what *about* romance? This was an anti-seduction scene; the seducer shoveling sugar down his throat, hacking, spitting, smoking. She looked over her shoulder, the lineup of men waiting to capitalize on his failure. She sensed their excitement; if Jerard had managed to kiss her, maybe one of them would achieve even more. Jerard was repulsive and yet somehow likable in that repulsiveness, a difficult combination to manage. It was almost comical. He was probably close to fifty, and she was not yet half that age. Desire was a problem for everyone; it was the uninvited guest on every dinner journey.

"No regrets about love?" he asked.

"What is this, the Age of Chivalry?" she laughed. "You do this out of habit; there's a woman, you try for her, to maintain your technique."

"You American women are cold, too independent. Why do you want to be alone?"

Jerard over the luxury of solitude? "I haven't had an adequate shower in weeks?" she offered. Why did she resist men? Why not pursue them, initiate sex, disseminate love? Anticipate and precede, turn a defense into an offense, flip the game around? She had a choice between Gustavo—attractive but thinly flavored—and Jerard— ugly, sophisticated, harsh. She wanted neither, or both, and having no choice left her open to accidents.

They piled back onto the jeep. Lili looked up the valley at the film of shapeless, gray clouds gathering and blunting the sun's warmth. Wazir gunned the engine and sped toward the bridge. There was a frightening cracking sound, the jeep dipping downward onto the planks, which trembled. It appeared as if they were crossing perfect, empty air. The pulsing of adrenaline through her body made Lili smile. She felt happy, in the midst of this clot of humanity, at risk. United in danger, connected by foolhardiness—none of this touched her heart with fear. Then, they were on the other side and the men were shouting in celebratory, looping cries. This was what she loved: movement, the passing terrain, the world unfolding around her.

They were the last to be dropped off, where the road ended at a sagging, two-story, adobe-and-wood house overlooking a field and a river. There was nothing but silence and pines climbing behind, all the way to the border with Afghanistan.

· Jerard embraced a stocky man wearing oversized pants and a boxy down jacket; castoffs from American clothing contributions to Afghani refugees who then sold them to make money. They spoke in French. "This is Abdul, and this is his, the Hotel Shangri-La." Jerard gestured at the run-down building.

Abdul had green eyes like translucent stones in the dark water of his face. He remained unsmiling as he opened a low door and motioned for them to enter. "There is food upstairs."

The room was cave-like, murky light coming through a single window covered with chicken wire and a sheet of opaque plastic. A dirt floor littered with cigarette butts and wrappers, three rope charpoys haphazardly placed so as not to touch the walls. There was no other furniture, no electricity, no heat.

"Abdul is a miserable hotelier," Jerard said. "I should have warned you."

Lili dropped her pack on the furthest charpoy and pulled out her sleeping bag. "It's awful, but I've got candles, and if it gets really cold we could build a fire on the floor." She busily pushed the bed into a straight line along the window, fluffed her bag, rummaged for her headlamp, matches, candles. She had an urge to sweep and arrange.

Gustavo shook his head. "Shangri-La?"

"Hey, I told you it wasn't real." Jerard sat on a charpoy, spooning sugar. "Abdul is the most important Kalash man in the valley. You know, the Kalash are descendants of Alexander the Great's army and they are not Muslim, right?"

Lili interrupted, "I'm going for a walk."

"Aren't you hungry?" Gustavo asked.

She made a face. "No more dal."

Both Gustavo and Jerard fell silent. "All right, come along if you want." It was like having puppies or children who couldn't let her go off alone. Which would she prefer: Gustavo's melancholy? Jerard's chatter?

Gustavo stayed to eat; Jerard stuffed his sugar back into his jacket pocket and said, "So," as if there had been no interruption. "Abdul is trying to help his people keep their culture and their land, but he's scattered."

Jerard continued to talk, but Lili didn't attend. They were in the woods, inhaling sharp air. "Listen," Lili said. The day had turned to wind, the trees swaying and humming, the river rumbling on a lower note. They picked their way among water-smoothed boulders beside the river, over browned leaves, crackling like eggshells. Lili regretted Jerard's company. True solitude was a rare pleasure, while that other solitude, being alone among strangers, had become everyday life.

"What's Gustavo's problem?" Jerard asked.

"He's sad. Maybe he's always like that." She felt Gustavo's sadness, bigger than himself, like a virus floating in the air; anyone could catch it. She suffered from it herself, though she wouldn't admit it, would hide it like a blemish on her face.

Icy white water curled around stones without cease. Nature didn't tire of repetition, and it made her aware of her impatience; she was incapable of staying in one place— she didn't even like to recross the same terrain. She breathed in the scent of pines, winter water, untouched earth. For the smell itself, it was a worthwhile journey.

"My mother, where do you live?" From nowhere a boy of about twelve appeared. He was thin with a narrow, serious face and slight shoulders.

Reluctant to hear the sound of her own voice, she said, "In the United States."

"Come to my house." It was a command rather than an invitation. The three walked in silence, until the boy held out his hand. "I am the son of a poor man. Give me ten rupees." She wanted to laugh, but he was too solemn.

"Here's a chocolate bar." She imitated his flat delivery, the soft commanding tones. From her inside jacket pocket she pulled out chocolate from China, which tasted like plastic but which she'd been saving for three months. "Where is Afghanistan?"

"Near." He put the chocolate bar in his pocket. Shortly, they entered a low stone building through a doorway of stiffened animal skins. A woman sat beside a thickly smoking fire with a baby in her lap. "My mother," the boy said. He dropped a goatskin on the dirt floor for Lili and Jerard.

Lili grasped the woman's rough hand and tried not to cough. The woman's face was a weave of wrinkles, her left eye blooming with a milky blue cataract. She spoke to Lili and the boy translated: "She says you are very healthy, young and strong. Not like her. Are you married to this man?"

"No." Unimaginable.

"Fool," Jerard whispered. "Now she's going to think you're a whore. I'll be your husband." He winked.

Lili's eyes were tearing from the smoke, and she blinked them fiercely.

The boy translated: "She says you should have a husband and babies. You should cook and weave and sew. Who is this man?"

Lili said, "A friend." Maybe. Husband and Babies. Cook and Sew. Life as Advanced Home Ec. She was unqualified, had barely passed home ec, never learned to make a piecrust, botched the apron she was meant to sew from a rice paper pattern.

The boy lifted a bent, burnt teakettle off the fire, rinsed out three cups, and poured water into them. The woman adjusted the baby in her lap. There were two bloated and blackened goatskins hanging in a corner of the room. There was a sack of flour, a teakettle, a large pot, a stack of bowls, an assortment of worn, carved wooden spoons, and several wide baskets. This was the woman's kitchen; there were no appliances, and soot was allowed to reign, coating everything in powdery black. In another corner was a pile of animal skins and wool blankets. A black and red weaving hung from a wall. All was arranged. In every country Lili visited, every village or city, she met people who thought she should be at home with a husband and children. They told her she was living the wrong kind of life. She wondered if she were a bad person, a confused person, a unique person. What kind of life was she trying to live? She sank into the warmth of the room, the smoke a soft cloak, and sipped the fog-colored tea the boy had given her. She imagined warm gray and white ashy flakes filling her lungs, feathering through her insides.

"My mother likes you; she says you should marry her son, my brother. He's a good man."

"Tell her I'm honored but I cannot get married today."

Everyone laughed. The boy continued translating: "Her daughter, my sister, has a husband, a bad man. My sister's first husband was beautiful, but he died of a sickness in his bones, and then nobody would marry her except this bad man."

The room fell silent.

"*Vamanos,*" Jerard said.

"I'm sorry about your sister. Thank you for the tea."

men had taken one of the carcasses outside, working through it with knives, their hands dark in the flesh. She picked up some meat and was surprised at its warmth, how close to life death was. It steamed in her palm, warming her chilled fingers. A moment of understanding beat in on her pulse but, like true understanding, it vanished. She looked up at the sky, an old gray blanket, wrapping the earth for the night, enfolding moon and stars. She felt embraced, held against massive boulders and furry trees, everything rounded and shadowed.

It began to snow, wet clumps sticking to tree branches, rocks, her jacket and boots. She walked through the blur of falling white, looking behind her, expecting someone to be on her heels, but she was alone. How deceptively soft the land seemed, almost cozy, almost warm. A great letting go, the snow falling and falling. By morning, the rocks and earth and tree stumps would disappear beneath rounding layers of white; the world would be smoothed. Light flakes melted on her cheeks, sliding down to her chin and her mouth. She tasted the chill of Pakistani snow.

The road would be closed, and they would be stuck here for days or weeks. Landlocked and snowbound with a couple of hot-breathed men. And the serious boy had invited her—ordered her—to return tomorrow for a visit. Here she was, in a village in Pakistan, with social obligations. She considered what she had that she could bring the boy and his mother: a Mao pin, a postcard of the Hollywood hills, a snail shell from the beach in Hong Kong, a deck of cards. Yes, the cards. And lotion for his mother's hands. Gustavo and Jerard would come, and she would teach everyone to play hearts. They would pass the long, snowy afternoons, trying to avoid hearts and the queen of spades.

She felt inadequate, heartless, vacant. How easy it was for a woman to become a reject; how near was the dangerous edge of a woman's life.

They got up to leave. "Where is Afghanistan?"

The boy stepped outside and turned, pointing. "That tree is Afghanistan. Come back tomorrow," he ordered.

Of course the landscape was the same in every direction; there was no possible way to determine a border. Lili walked to the tree, a tall sugar pine, and inhaled its sweet smell. She let her cheek rest against the bark, her feet cushioned in pine needles, and stood still, mind alert, tuned to the sounds of the wind fluttering over this border, the feel of herself in this other country, the smell of wet pine. She felt the same in Afghanistan or Pakistan, her self, her thorny complications traveled with her.

"You've been invited to a wedding celebration," Abdul said after knocking on the door to their room at the Shangri-La.

"We are strangers," Gustavo said.

"You are my guests," Abdul said. "OK, OK."

The temperature had risen, the wind stilled, and the sky paled with thick clouds. They picked their way down the rock-strewn road.

"Going to a wedding," Jerard sang. "Gustavo, have you been married?"

"Maybe I will marry my girlfriend."

"We'll take that as a no. Lili, we know, would not marry unless there were sufficient lust. No, she is too pure. She will never marry." He laughed.

"Have *you* been married?" Gustavo asked.

"Three glorious times and divorced three times. I have three children—I think they are in Italy or France, I'm not sure."

"Do you miss them?" Lili asked.

"I don't know them very well."

"Why marry so many times?" Gustavo asked.

Jerard snorted his laugh. "Because the women wanted it, of course, and I would have been a fool to disagree. For me, one woman is insufficient. So, there were problems."

"You were not faithful?" Gustavo asked.

"I never promise fidelity."

Gustavo nodded. "There are so many women." He sighed heavily. "I always meet women I like."

"Like Lili. We all like Lili." Jerard took hold of Lili's elbow. "You're our fairy woman, even if you have no sense of romance," Jerard said. Gustavo put his arm through her other arm.

"I still love my wives. Those were wonderful years." Jerard stroked Lili's fingers.

And Gustavo pressed close. Fine. How could romance and love flourish in a place without electricity, heat, mirrors, or hot showers?

"Why don't you get married, Lili?" Jerard asked.

"You're like a dog, chasing the same ball hour after hour. Ask Gustavo—he's not married."

"I want to get married," Gustavo said with energy, "but maybe I can't be faithful."

"Gustavo answers the question, at least," Jerard said.

She didn't understand marriage, like a language for which there was no phrase book. All the impenetrable doubts she had about coupling. "People say, 'I want to get married and have three children,'" Lili said. "I say, I want to grow African violets, make feta cheese, live in fourteen different countries. Why is life always reduced to mating?"

Gustavo laughed, louder than they'd ever heard from him. Jerard sighed. "Mating, my dear, is the elemental.

Violets and goat cheese, yes, that's nice. But ecstasy and suffering? That's living."

When they arrived at the wedding, Abdul explained in a quick whisper, "Two weddings: two sisters. Downstairs they will sacrifice four goats and a cow, for good marriages. They eat and dance all night. We go upstairs first, to eat."

The men went upstairs, but Lili entered the stable below, orange firelight flickering over the skittish shapes of four goats. Smoke drifted through the closely packed people. Men took up bundles of pine chips, then lit and held them as torches until their fingers were nearly caught in the flames. One man wielded a wide, long blade, casting the shadow of a giant's sword against the ceiling. The cow ate placidly from a pile of hay in a corner. The man with the blade stepped forward, and another man grabbed one of the goats. He swung and slit the goat's throat, then quickly, the other three. There were high-pitched grunts as they died. The men strung the goats from the beams, their blood draining into a stone trough. A man reached into a goat and pulled out the coils of intestines, the clots of liver and kidney, slapping them into a pile of straw, his arm red past his elbow.

Slaughter: a violent word wrapped in a halo of smoke, dipped in a pool of blood, rich with the stink of organs. Just because she had grown up in the suburbs, had never witnessed more than the killing of spiders, ants, and mosquitoes, didn't mean that she could turn all of this into something exotically significant; tell stories of ceremonial sacrifice for the entertainment of people who ate salmon filets and canapés at their weddings, who bought their plastic-wrapped meat in refrigerated sections of fluorescent-lit supermarkets. Marriage, death, sacrifice, celebration. She pushed out of the room into sharp cold, past a group of girls singing softly on some stairs. The

Pilgrims

FRANCES MELLON WASN'T ABOUT TO tell her husband she hated China. Hated its narrow alleys and wide boulevards, all of them cramped and festering with human life beneath the tasteless, drab architecture that was the banner of communism; hated its rivers, percolating with rank pollutants; hated the obsequious smile of socialism slathered over every greedy capitalist enterprise; hated the pinching, shrill tourist hustlers and the sullen uniformed army of clerks and waiters who watched her as if she were a freak, an abomination, a scourge on the politically correct surface of their precious Middle Kingdom; hated the gobs of germ-laden spit expectorated on every promenade, in hallways and vestibules; hated the dishes of slithery food, and the fact that she had to eat these indigestible meals using two sticks, surely an overly complicated means of executing a very ordinary activity. But Donald was her best friend and husband of thirty-eight years. This trip was as important to him as their wedding, the births of their children, and the fifteen-foot marlin he'd caught off the coast of San Diego. So, she did her best. She didn't count the days remaining, didn't sink into a depression the way some women would, didn't complain. She was fiercely cheerful. She gave Donald and every Chinese person they met the best of her even-tempered, pragmatic, patient, attentive nature.

She heard Donald awaken before the alarm and click it off. He'd been capable of doing this ever since she'd been sleeping with him. How lucky she was to have someone to preserve the morning quiet. He said the unexpected shriek of an alarm was a terrible awakening, like having your heart slammed into a stone.

"Five o'clock, Fran," he said as he rose and went into the bathroom. They were in a three-star hotel midway up Mt. Emei, in Sichuan Province, though three stars seemed to mean that the carpets were badly stained and unvacuumed—cellophane wrappers and bits of candy in the corners, cigarette ash just around the edge of the bed.

Today they were hiking up the mountain, one of China's four sacred Buddhist peaks. Fran thought it might rain all day and they wouldn't see anything when they got to the top, *if* they got to the top. Her worries had buzzed like a persistent mosquito all night, leaving her irritable and droopy. While she dressed and packed a few things for their overnight at a monastery on the mountain, she reviewed the worries, setting them in order. She was worried about going without a guide, which Donald had pooh-poohed. "It's only one night, Fran, and I listened to those language tapes. It will be fun for me to rely on my Chinese. I think I can do it; I *want* to do it." But it didn't seem right to her that their guide was suddenly shirking his duties—clearly, in her mind, skittish about climbing the mountain.

She was worried that it would be too much for Donald. He'd had a desk job and liked sedentary activities: fishing, bridge, chess. And then, too, he might be disappointed and turn glum and moody. She was worried about their accommodations; if three-star hotels were this grubby, what would a monastery halfway up a mountain be like? Not that she required excesses of comfort—they had done some camping when they were first married—but she drew the line at rats, bedbugs, lice. Donald had chosen the monastery, and they would take a van to it from the top, returning to the hotel the following day. As far as she knew, Donald had never stayed at a monastery in his life, and she didn't know where this sudden interest in Buddhism came from. His parents, after all, had come to China to convert Buddhists to Christians.

And the monkeys, of course; she was worried about the monkeys.

Tomorrow, she told herself, it will all be over.

Before seven they were penetrating the misty green flank of the mountain, paying their special, inflated-for-foreigners entrance fee to a sleepy attendant. *You pay to suffer,* Fran thought, *and that's important because it reminds you that you've chosen this activity.*

It didn't feel like a mountain, just an aimless stone path through a narrow, green valley dense with bamboo, feathery conifers, and dripping leaves. Fran was nervously alert, turning at every rustle and twitter. Donald carried the daypack with their overnight things and a water bottle, but no food. She carried a thin bamboo walking stick, to ward off monkeys. She'd removed her watch, wedding band, and the gold earrings that had been her grandmother's. Like preparing for a religious ritual, stripping yourself of material possessions.

Their map claimed: "Droves of monkeys, frolicking in the mountain or by the roadside, give added interest to the tourists." But Fran, in charge of guidebooks and research, knew better. The monkeys reputedly attacked foreign tourists while leaving Chinese tourists and locals alone; they picked through pockets, ripped away jewelry, tore open or ran off with backpacks. There was a blurry picture on their map of a gray, wild-haired thing with a squashed rat's face, perched on the shoulders of a frightened-looking tourist, thin, furred fingers gripping the innocent human head.

Probably her worries were unfounded. Focus on the pleasures: squawk and chirp of birds; dense greenery, filigreed and glistening with dew; soft trickle of a stream. Bright white clouds drifted open and then closed like curtains, exposing tantalizing flashes of blue sky. She followed Donald, forcing herself into a quiet that seemed rare in China, not to mention the clean air. She inhaled deeply. Donald was here. Everything was going to be fine.

Donald, steady and quick in the midst of trouble, couldn't attend to *potential* dangers; he didn't anticipate and deflect. Unlike her brothers—physically fit, competent men who were detailed planners—Donald was impractical, his head apt to be absorbed in abstractions. He was a daydreamer. How many times they'd almost been in car wrecks because he was probably in China. She never knew where he might be. Or, if she strayed in her vigilance while navigating, they would be lost, sometimes in dangerous neighborhoods. And Donald, driving slowly, door unlocked, head craning out the open window trying to catch a street sign, as if they weren't a couple of middle-class people in a clean, late-model sedan passing a street corner full of men drinking wine from paper bags.

"I enjoyed dinner last night," Donald said. Their guide had ordered a special pre-climbing meal, perhaps celebrating his escape from the climb.

"Yes, it was thoughtful of him to do that for us." Fran didn't want to recall the weird and awful-tasting things she'd tried to eat.

"Chen is shifty, but likeable."

"Mmm." Mr. Chen, their guide, was a caricature of Oriental inscrutability; he always seemed to be saying one thing while secretly meaning another. Fran wouldn't trust him with her spare change.

"I haven't had a chance to tell you this, but I had the most wonderful memory when we were in Chengdu," Donald said.

She yawned. China memories were like a movie that never ended, a movie whose plot and meaning she had never figured out, though she knew the main characters.

"When we were walking down those narrow back streets near the river, remember those old people sitting on low stools, playing Chinese chess and bridge?"

"Yes." And the smell of rotting vegetables and fermenting something or other, something rancid and bitter that burned at the back of her throat. And a woman placidly snapping the necks of doves, piling them neatly, one pale gray, soft body on top of another.

"I remembered the old woman I used to see with bound feet. I don't know how old I was when I first saw her, six or eight maybe. My dad sent me out to buy something at the market and she sat in this alley that I passed through, on one of those same low stools. Her stringy gray hair seemed to be half-attached to her scalp. You could see these bare patches. She was round and small. Probably she thought I was a cute foreign boy; I felt sorry for her. I accepted the stalk of sugar cane she offered me, but was afraid to eat it. Her eyes were murky—maybe she had cataracts—and her face wrinkled and smooth at once, powdery and puffy. I stood looking at her; the Chinese were never ashamed to look if they were curious, and I hadn't learned yet that staring was rude, though I think my parents were trying to teach me. Then she stretched her legs out, stiffly, and made a low, almost imperceptible sound. I saw her feet, no larger than my hand, and I was shocked. It was the first time I'd seen bound feet, and I hadn't heard anything about them, and I didn't under-stand how she could have such things at the end of her legs. Just these pointy miniature black slippers. They fright-ened me, and I couldn't stop looking at them. When I finally glanced up at her face, I saw something in her eyes. I didn't know what it meant at the time. But now. She was proud of her tiny feet, but there was also bitterness and regret."

He stopped talking, and Fran heard the slight rasping of his breathing. "This is"—he paused to breathe—"what I find fascinating about China."

Who *was* this person, dragging her up a mountain in the middle of China, oblivious to the dangers awaiting them? Oh, she *knew* Donald, like those Russian wooden dolls, one inside the other; Donald was inside her and she was inside him over and over again. She loved him, like a benediction, like a penance. Their bodies had so fused with repeated familiarity that touch was about as erotic as kneading cold, stiff dough; his voice spoke in her head from the same place as her own. Still, it was just, well, what? She sighed. "What do you think it is about China, exactly, that has such a powerful appeal for you?" If this were *her* trip, motivated by *her* past, you can bet her reasons would be typed and filed and ready for anyone to peruse.

"Oh, honey, I don't know. It's just so *different*, I guess." She felt like a game show host pushing that buzzer— *Blech! Mr. Mellon, I'm sorry, you can't win our 1998 Chevy Blazer with* that *answer. Next contestant please.* But, she wasn't being honest; she was as fond of his vague dreaminess as she was exasperated by it. These moments reminded her that she was distinct, different from Donald. In her daydreams she planned meals, vacations, routes for the next day's errands. Sometimes Donald seemed to her like a novel, something she understood on the surface, but beneath that surface were layers of feelings and motives that were out of focus, that she could not penetrate.

They came to a bridge lined with benches on which rested a couple of peasants with bulky bundles strapped to their backs. They were languidly feeding the fifteen or so monkeys that squatted about, sleepily eating, scratching, nibbling. Donald strode forward full of charm and chatter, trying to whip up a conversation with the peasants, who merely stared at him. Either they didn't understand his accent, they didn't understand Mandarin, they were pretending ignorance, or they were incapable of believing that a foreigner could speak Chinese.

Frances walked rapidly, purposefully, not looking left or right, though she was acutely aware of monkeys turning and lifting their heads as she passed, their pinched, unwashed faces, those flickering, curious eyes, the frame of stubby, unkempt hair. Her heart was beating unpleasantly fast, her pulse pounding as if her wrists and throat were constricting her.

She was almost over the bridge, almost past the monkeys. A large monkey. Distracted by the sight of this hefty male, she didn't see the small one that ran after her and pinched her leg, gave her pants a tug. Playful or malicious? She hopped and shrieked, rushing forward.

"What?"

"That monkey just pinched my leg." She didn't stop striding, bumping into Donald, who had turned around. He was hindering her getaway. *Get away, get away.*

"It was only playing. They won't do anything. Slow down."

"You don't know what you're talking about." He hadn't read the guidebooks. "You think you know everything about China because you lived here sixty years ago when it was a completely different place! And you were seven years old or something." She felt like shaking him.

"Fran," he said, his voice like a soft rag, polishing her surfaces, delivering a litany of meaningless words. She sighed. Here was the familiar voice of her husband, falling around her like water, and she was soothed, against her judgment.

Long flights of stone steps snaked up through the foliage; now they were climbing in earnest. Her legs ached slightly, her breathing was audible but regular. Six hours of StairMaster, except these Chinese steps were treacherous: wet, slick, uneven. She couldn't set her legs to a rhythm and then daydream; each step required her full attention.

They reached a clearing with a sign that read: "Caution! Monkeys About. Stay Alert!"

"Well," Frances exhaled in something like a gasp. She felt the sign justified her fears, though it also made her pulse race.

"Fine, we'll be alert then, won't we now?" Donald said, as if he were talking to one of their grandchildren. "Don't let this worry of yours get out of hand. I know how you can be."

"Don't patronize me."

"Don't overreact."

Their silence was tense, familiar. "Anyway, since when are you afraid of monkeys?" Donald asked.

"Today," she said. Stupid question; when could she have encountered monkeys, except safely behind bars in a zoo?

He wanted to know why. "I don't know," she said, feeling a little bubble of hysteria within her. Was she being irrational and fainthearted? Wild animals and human beings should leave each other alone; they were not of the same culture, the same species.

They continued to climb, and nothing happened, though Fran was not reassured or lulled. When was the last time she'd felt afraid like this? Maybe never; how predictable and solid her life was, full of routine, doors that locked, domesticated pets. She organized arguments against her anxiety; they were on an expensive, private tour of China. What bad things could happen if you spent a lot of money? Money bought safety and security, right?

A trailside tea shed sold soft drinks, cheap souvenirs, snacks, and monkey food, which annoyed Fran, this encouragement of inappropriate interaction between humans and monkeys. They stepped into the courtyard of the first temple on their route, Fairy Peak Temple: sagging rooflines, chipped paint, overgrown weedy gardens. Three monks slumped sullenly on some steps, hunched around a transistor radio, fiddling with the dial until they found a scratchy pop tune. *Not exactly a bastion of spirituality,* Frances thought. And it hardly looked habitable, which didn't make the evening any more appealing than the present. She needed something to look forward to. She glanced at Donald, but he was smiling, grimly positive. She knew his thoughts: they were having a good time, an adventurous time, damn it. Maybe he was right. Maybe she was completely missing the point of China. Doubt ratcheted through her, and she stumbled.

At a rest platform with mist like a flung scarf round the trees, they met a young Swedish couple.

"Hallo," the boy cried. "It's very steep, isn't it?" He looked like he was in high school but he probably was in his twenties. He was big and blond and hearty. He and Donald fell into a back-slapping joking fest with a kind of frantic glee. Frances hung back, slightly embarrassed by her husband's exuberance.

Then the girl, pretty, also blond and fit, said, "Have you seen monkeys?"

"Yes, at the bridge."

"Did you talk to the monks at the last monastery? They told us there's a male who is so large and aggressive they have to beat him off with a long, heavy pole. They showed us the pole."

"Oh, dear," Frances said.

Donald looked at her severely.

"And here's our defense." The boy laughed nervously and waved their slender walking stick, exactly like the one Frances had.

"The monks are quite afraid of this monkey," the girl said.

"That sounds like a sensible reaction," Frances said, avoiding looking at Donald.

"If it's even true," Donald said. "They were probably just pulling your leg."

Both the boy and girl smiled politely, but said nothing.

"That's an expression, an idiom."

Oh, God, he was going to explain.

"It means, maybe they were teasing you, to make you afraid, you know?"

Frances smiled into the silence. "You better go first," she said. "You'll pass us in no time anyway."

After the Swedish couple left, Donald sat on a bench. "Let's rest for a minute longer."

She had an urge for petty argument, to push him, to sink her fist into the dense meat of his bicep. "Shall I rub your shoulders?" she asked. Maybe she'd make a pitch for him to start a regular exercise program, but then she saw the distant look of daydream in his eyes.

"I should have come back sooner," he said. "Or, maybe never."

Fran held her breath in a moment that felt like a shattered windshield. He didn't explain. What she imagined was that the great beauty of his past was proving to be ordinary, maybe even ugly. Well. *The Fall of China.* And she felt the sadness, the impossibility of ever going back, the relentless demand that life move forward, and forward. Toward what?

"We better keep going," he said.

At least they still had secrets; how would she live without her stash of private thoughts – a realm no one saw or imagined?

It began to rain. Donald suggested lunch and chose a dank, filthy, trailside food stall that didn't look as if anything edible could issue from its medieval kitchen. Fran swirled her chopsticks through the greasy noodles without protest. She couldn't have lifted them with chopsticks if she'd wanted to, and she didn't want to. Instead, she watched the water leak through the patchboard plank roof and listened to Donald happily discussing the World Cup with the cook in Chinese.

"I miss noodles like this," he said. Fran stared at the shine of grease on his chin. He couldn't just keep eating one oily meal after another without suffering some adverse effects. Didn't he have any sense of the proximity of death?

"I'll buy a couple of those rain parkas," he said. They were only flimsy sheets of plastic—wouldn't even hold up as a garbage bag. But Donald was triumphant that he got them for the Chinese price, by asking the cook ahead of time how much they cost. The vendor, who wanted to charge three times as much, was furious, and Fran couldn't blame him. Donald's delight was distasteful, inappropriate. *Let them rip us off,* she thought. *They need the money, and we* are *foolish tourists, and the money* is *nothing to us.* He was like an adult winning a game against a child. Fran hid her embarrassment and dutifully wrapped herself in the tissue like a sheath.

Her husband. She remembered how charming Donald's stories of life in China had seemed to her when they first met, and his aura of exoticism; he could speak Chinese, he could eat anything with chopsticks: spaghetti, peas. He was a person with a history, to whom things had already happened, while her life was pending, events worth telling about waiting in the wings of her fate.

Only after they were married did she realize that Donald was going to tell those stories to everyone they met, and she was sentenced to a lifetime of listening to him talk about China. She hadn't expected married life to include exotic travel, or life in other countries. She had married Donald because he seemed spacious on the inside, with a different kind of awareness of himself and the world. China had, at least in part, made him who he was, so she settled into listening to the reel of his China memories, played again and again.

When Sylvia and Peter, their two eldest, had suggested a retirement trip to China for them, Fran took to the idea. She wanted to see what it was that had occupied Donald's affections for so many years. They could afford it, since Donald had shown himself to be an astute investor. But it had been put off for a year, and then another six months. Eventually, Fran began to feel that Donald didn't want to return, didn't want to risk his memories.

"They're called pilgrims," Fran told Donald as she read from the guidebook. "And they climb the mountain every year for longevity." Pilgrims, as in *The Canterbury Tales*. But they didn't seem worthy of literature, only a bunch of wrinkled, shrunken old women, hunkered down in the Mahayana Temple, the second temple on their route, out of the rain, away from the two wide-shouldered, menacing monkeys stalking the rooftops, holding everyone beneath hostage. Fran kept looking up at the monkeys circling the courtyard rooftop, her fear making her mouth sour. She forced her attention into the temple. Short women in boxy, navy blue pants and jackets wandered about in a flurry of feminine bustle, praying and lighting candles, bowing and chatting. The mixture of gossip and reverence was oddly soothing, like a beauty parlor in a church. Fran, at 5'11", was a giant among them, the big monkey. She peered into one of the dorm rooms where women napped and knitted, like a retirement home. Fran was repulsed and envious. It seemed peaceful and warm, but also heavy with fatigue and damp decay. No amount of lighting candles and climbing mountains could prevent death, though she admired the calm that emanated from these women. Perhaps the mountain did have a kind of sacred power.

They exited through the back of the temple compound,

entering a brown, soupy landscape of dripping trees laced with a grayish green fog. It was so quiet they could hear the rain hitting leaves, like a leaking tap. Fran found herself violently wishing for the end, for it all to be over with. She had no tolerance for, no practice being, fearful. She wanted to weep hard enough to wash away the grittiness of anxiety.

At a bend in the path, Donald stopped abruptly and whispered, "Monkeys." He opened his arms, exposing the innocent, white flesh of his palms. "Show them you have nothing to offer." He walked carefully forward, in surrender, as if someone were holding a gun to his head that might go off if he misstepped. Frances stood immobilized on the stone path; she was a mannequin without blood or muscle or bone as she watched one of the monkeys jump onto Donald's daypack, while the other two began tugging on it from the bottom. Donald was being pulled backward, struggling to stand upright as the three monkeys worked to get the daypack for themselves. One of them sank its talon-like fingers into Donald's sparse hair.

"The stick, the stick," Donald said, waving his arms, trying to bend forward against the pull of the monkeys.

Action, oh God. She edged forward and flailed the stick at the monkeys, tapped it on the stones near them, hearing the light *tap tap* with a panicked cynicism. What a pitiful defense, what a frail counterattack, and her insides shrank and quivered at her inability, with feeble weapon, and feebler nerves, to be sufficiently tough and aggressive. In an instant, the monkeys turned from Donald to her, their challenger. The scrunched flesh of their faces surrounded by dirty gray hair; those yellowed, needle teeth and the dark maws behind, from the depths of which emerged a hissing sound, slicing down her spine in a single paralyzing shiver.

"Oh!" She recoiled, as if she could curl herself into insignificance, invisibility, taking the ridiculous stick with her. "Give me the stick; you go." Now that the monkeys were off his back, Donald was calm.

She shoved the stick across to him, relieved to be rid of an item that seemed to be a problem more than a solution. But in order to pass Donald, she had to step forward, toward the monkeys who perched, tense, awaiting her move. Their squat bodies ready to leap, their little hands as agile and dexterous as her own. How far could they leap and how fast? What would they tear at with those simian digits?

"Fran."

"I can't."

Donald didn't chastise her or goad or coach her; he knew that she would eventually motivate herself and that was the best thing to do—let her do it herself. His patience, his knowledge of her character warmed her chest, eased her breathing slightly.

Best not to think. In an instant, she bolted forward, then flipped a quick turn up the next set of steps and up and up. She felt wonderfully coordinated, fit and light, swift and strong. It was exhilarating. At the second landing, she stopped and felt, then, her breath coming in full, hard gasps, each deep breath filling her with the hot flush of life. Not bad for an old lady, she thought.

A minute or two later, Donald appeared, wheezing slightly, coughing and gasping and unsteady. "I can't," he exhaled like a piston under pressure, "keep up with you when you're afraid of monkeys."

His pink and sweating face, labored breathing. Dear God, what if he had a heart attack on this mountain? Her large, florid husband; men didn't feel compelled to stay in good shape. She felt angry at him: he needed to exercise, eat less. And it would be nice to see that he wanted to look good for her, that he wanted to be attractive for his wife. Didn't he know younger men flirted with her? Didn't he pay attention? To him, their marriage was as unshakeable as this mountain.

"Do you feel all right? You rest, and I'll watch to see they don't come up the steps." But she could hardly stay put, edging up another couple of steps to keep the distance between herself and the monkeys.

"I'm fine."

The monkeys sleuthed after them, pausing as if they weren't really going anywhere. "We'll go slow and steady. Are you okay?"

"Yes." She was afraid, could feel the adrenaline scraping through her veins like caustic paint remover. She cringed at the image of those furry agile fingers, pulling on Donald's daypack, fiddling with the clips and straps. Monkeys should not have any interest in people; they should sensibly stay out of each other's way; they were too different, and also not different enough.

"They are quite fierce, very strong," Donald said, impressed.

He could praise anything Chinese.

They met a few unhappy mother monkeys forlornly cradling babies against their dirty, pink chests. Fran recognized the emotions in their disconcertingly human faces; they were stuck in the rain with the kids while Dad was off terrorizing passing tourists and they felt miserable and neglected. But monkeys always lived outside in the rain, and she didn't know if they mated for life, and she resented that she'd been caught anthropomorphizing those dreadful creatures.

Where the trail met the road, about three kilometers from the top, they had to walk a gauntlet of kiosks selling everything from plastic laughing Buddhas, the laugh so harsh and unpleasant it made you want to smash the Buddha to the ground, to umbrellas and heavy green Chinese army coats. It was a horror scene of commercialism, and Fran was embarrassed by the ugly, secular mess of things. What did the pilgrims make of this nonsense? China was bone without marrow, façade without substance. One minute you thought China was going to deliver something genuine, the next you felt duped, your hopeful expectations thrown down with a hoot and holler.

They were tired and the weather was bad and they forsook the top.

They ate dinner outside, under a portico, sitting on low stools at a dark, wooden table at the Temple of Ten Thousand Years, the oldest surviving monastery on the mountain. Their room, musty and soggy with humidity, was on the second floor of an old wooden building, trees out the window, the sound of birds, no monkeys. The toilets were down a rickety set of stairs and across a courtyard, with an outdoor trough for a sink. Clusters of pilgrims caroused, as if they were on a holiday weekend rather than a spiritual pilgrimage. It was late for dinner in China, nearly seven, and Fran and Donald were the only diners.

None of the dishes that came were what Donald had ordered.

"What's this? I ordered spicy and sour cucumbers and . . ." He turned to the waiter and delivered his complaints, waving his hands for emphasis. The waiter shrugged, indifferent.

Fran was relieved; the dishes not only looked fresh, but they were the most ordinary foods she'd seen yet: scrambled eggs and tomatoes, cabbage, spinach. No weird mushrooms, no eel or unchewable jellyfish, no animal parts that no one should eat. "Honey, this looks delicious."

"It looks like something we'd eat at home," Donald said, unhappy.

"Well, the ingredients are familiar, but the style is still Chinese. Come on, we've had a long day and we need food." Fran went through the motions of breaking apart the set of discardable chopsticks and rubbing them together to smooth out any splinters. Donald began picking delicately from the steaming oblong platters and his bowl of rice.

As usual, within a minute, Fran was frustrated. She couldn't get her chopsticks to collect enough egg and rice for a mouthful; most of what she hoped to bring to her mouth fell away before the chopsticks were close to her chin. The silly sticks wobbled and she tightened her grip on them, but the food slithered and slipped, and she was managing to feed herself very badly. She considered picking up one of the large serving spoons and spooning down impolite quantities of rice and egg and cabbage.

"You know, for an athlete, you sure are uncoordinated with those things. Let me show you." Donald's voice was warm and patient, the joking tone meant to let her know that he didn't regard her as entirely incompetent.

"But, you've shown me before."

"I can show you again, dear." He held up one chopstick. "Start with the bottom stick like this—you can get a very firm grip on it between your thumb and the fourth finger. Now take the second one between the thumb, first, and third finger, and that's the one that moves. The bottom one stays steady, the top does the grabbing. That looks better already."

Her imitation of his movements was half-hearted, imperfect. He was so tolerant, devoid of judgment and criticism; he thought she was wonderful and nothing she could do ever shook that. But she felt an unreasonable hatred and dislike—she couldn't stand that he asked her, over and over again, to befriend, to love and admire a place that had preoccupied him, for no good reason, for most of their lives. She hated him for pushing her into the arms of China again and again. She wanted to eat with a fork and knife and spoon; she didn't want to be adept with chopsticks.

Fran hadn't slept well. The bed was clammy, the floors creaked as if people were pacing, and through the walls she could hear conversations in Chinese. Then, just as she was falling asleep, gongs had reverberated through the trees. The deep, mournful sounds nearly made her weep, for what she didn't know, but when she rose, very early, she had a feeling of having been washed on her insides— not scrubbed clean, just a deep rinsing.

She dressed quietly and went downstairs, across the courtyard to the toilets. The morning was a flat, steel gray, dark figures like cutouts of the night: the Chinese stayed up late and awoke early. She splashed her face in the water at the trough and then decided to have a look around the grounds of the monastery, which seemed, in this lightening hour, peaceful.

The gardens were cared for, but a natural messiness and chaos were allowed, everything pleasantly ragged. There was an impressive variety of shrubs and trees and flowering plants, not many of which she recognized. She wandered through courtyards, past ponds with lily pads, and peered into buildings, full of images of Buddha. One building held a statue of a man—who was he?—sitting atop a gigantic white elephant. It was nice to look at these things, but they meant nothing to her; she might as well have been looking at engine parts, and she felt dissatisfied with herself for not paying better attention, for willfully knowing nothing about China.

At the back of the monastery compound was a two-story wooden building with a wide veranda running its length. This must be the monks' quarters, for she saw an old monk sitting on a rattan couch, his thickly slippered feet propped on a settee. He was wrapped in a heavy, long robe and his chin was sunk, with his wispy beard splayed across his chest. He prayed quietly, beads slipping through his fingers like liquid. Other monks strolled in soft shoes that made no noise, hands clasped behind their backs, calm and meditative. But it was the old man Fran watched, as he sat, well-tended and ignored, engrossed in his inner life, as if the great, roiling mess of China didn't matter. He seemed to her like a pin on the map of the world, marking a place, a real place. She felt the expanse of this awful, mysterious country surging in waves away from this old man, praying in a language she didn't understand. How little she knew. She knew nothing of China, had understood nothing about this trip, hadn't looked behind or beneath or beyond. She felt overcome with loss, of what she wasn't sure. The desire to weep piled like stones in the bowl of her chest. The monk blurred while she stood very still, attending to the pile of stones in her chest, trying to keep them from toppling.

Foreign Relations

ON HER FIFTH MORNING IN TASHKENT, Vicki was drying her face and hands at the bathroom sink when Olga poked her head in from the kitchen and jabbed her index finger through the air, cranking away in Russian. Olga's cartoon mouth blew a bubble of symbols and exclamation points. Vicki didn't understand a word, but she understood everything. Olga was telling her she was drying her face wrong. Proving the translation accurate, Olga snatched the towel and patted Vicki's face with it. How it should be done. Vicki shook her head in awe at Olga's audacity. She was a guest of Olga's country, in Olga's apartment. She was a foreigner, a grown woman with a profession and a husband, but Olga treated her like an untrained household pet, minus the customary lavish affection.

Vicki escaped to the toilet closet; the toilet was on a raised platform in a small box of a room. When she sat down, her knees practically touched the door despite her short legs. The room was icy with a sweetish smell—air freshener but not fresh. Her life lacked dialogue; she hardly spoke while Olga and Misha spoke copiously but didn't listen. They were bad background music Vicki wanted to turn off.

Don't forget to put the paper into the basket next to the toilet. She worried that she'd forget in the middle of the night, drop the paper, gray and wrinkly like elephant skin, down the toilet, and the plumbing would back up and ice cold toilet water would flood the apartment and Olga and Misha would shriek at her. Because in Tashkent, toilet paper couldn't go down the toilet—a deep, funnel-shaped aperture, far away and dark at the bottom, not like the shallow white porcelain of American Standards where everything disappeared from the sparkling bowl in a single efficient evacuation.

It had been like this since her arrival. Vicki told herself they were concerned for her well-being in their country, but she wanted to yell back at them, "I am a first-rate economic consultant. Your government officials have invited me to advise them on how to change to a capitalist economy. I'm forty-one years old, I earn $150,000 a year, drive a car, speak French, make my own bread, use a computer." None of which Olga could do.

After her lecture and demonstration on how to dry oneself properly with a towel, Olga went to get dressed for work, leaving Vicki alone with Olga's retired husband. Misha set out breakfast, no questions asked, no preferences inquired after. Was this how they treated their grown son? There were two soft-boiled eggs, a bowl of thick sour cream, watery jam, dense bread and butter. When Vicki tried to eat the bread plain or with only a thin layer of butter, Misha grabbed it from her with contempt and slabbed on butter like sliced cheese. She hated eggs any style. Yolk seemed like something left over from prehistory, certainly not an edible item. She thought of placentas, of afterbirth.

She began by splitting the eggs in two and loosening the firm white flesh from the shell with a single scoop of the spoon, letting the steam curl into the small kitchen, heated with the four gas burners lit. Then she ate the bread slowly, waiting for Misha to leave to get a magazine or cough in the living room. The minute he was gone, she opened the kitchen window and tilted the eggs out into the snow six floors below. They dropped soundlessly and disappeared, not a trace of yellow. She felt a thrill of anxiety that Olga and Misha would find a yellow puddle of preserved yolk in the spring mud and would collapse over her ungratefulness. She flushed with adrenaline and pleasure at the sight of the successfully emptied shells. How pathetic; she was resorting to such absurd subterfuge over food.

She had tried to tell them. No, she *had* told them, using her Russian phrase book, that she didn't like eggs, thank you. Russian had a complicated grammar; she dreaded learning about declensions, which sounded like a painful dental procedure. But she could pronounce the words, had learned the alphabet, and followed the sentence patterns in the book. *I don't like eggs, thank you* was not a complicated sentence. They didn't care; she should eat eggs.

Well, in Vicki's opinion, they should not eat eggs. Misha was sixty-six years old and looked like he was seventy-five. He smoked and coughed, pounding his sunken chest like a jar that wouldn't open. The bags of skin beneath his eyes were full and poochy, mirroring the downward slope of his sagging stomach. He had chest pains every day but insisted on walking her to the bus stop, down dangerously iced walkways and up a small incline, where he stopped, breathing heavily. She was terrified he was going to have a heart attack and she would be standing beside his prone body bedded in snow, frantically trying to find the words for *doctor, ambulance,* and *help* in her phrase book.

Olga had high blood pressure. Her face was red, she complained of headaches, and she got worked up over small details like how Vicki dressed to go out. Misha was going to have a heart attack, Olga was going to have a stroke, and Vicki was going to be stuck in that fetid apartment with a couple of half-dead people who would probably be shouting at her even as they gasped for breath. She tried to remember her CPR training, so far in the past, and then she caught herself. She should be concentrating on learning Russian and on adjusting to life in Uzbekistan instead of worrying about the health of a couple of cantankerous old people.

Vicki said she could walk to the bus stop alone, she could figure out how to get to the art museum, she could use the subway system. She waved her phrase book in front of them. Olga wagged her finger in Vicki's face, shouting in Russian. Vicki didn't understand a word, but she understood everything. Olga buttoned Vicki's coat, standing in the hallway, yanking it tight around her neck, tucked in her scarf, and rearranged her hat. Vicki was a kinked hose with the water on, words pooling inside of her. She wanted to tell Olga that if she chose to go out without her coat buttoned, it was a conscious and intelligent act on her part. But if she yelled back at Olga, she was falling into the trap of behaving like an adolescent.

Adults didn't have to declare their adultness; it was evident. So she said nothing, and stood, full of terror, rage, the desire to be polite, and admiration for Olga's force of character. Vicki couldn't remember the last time she had felt so impotent. Her real life in San Francisco seemed distant, spatially and temporally. Fifteen years, *swoosh,* shoveled out of sight. She wasn't surprised that she didn't miss Greg, but that didn't mean she knew what to do about it. Occasionally, no, regularly when she was home, she awoke in the middle of the night and wondered, *Who is this man?* Under the covers his curved form was like Florida cocked against the Gulf of Mexico, places she was uninterested in. *My husband,* she answered, *Greg.* Who *was* that? Her mother thought that they'd never had children because Greg's biking had made him sterile. They'd been together for fifteen years, married for thirteen. He taught high school history, studied permaculture in his free time, and had placed in ten of the hardest mountain-bike races in the western U.S. Greg was a good man. He seemed to be, anyway. Was it possible to ever really know another person? Greg said to her, "I know you," and if she had hackles, they would rise. As if she were already an event come and gone, history, definable, knowable. At forty-one, for God's sake.

She had urges to lift up carpets and rummage through the back of her closet searching for whatever was gone. Did it disappear, or go into hiding or travel somewhere else? What was it anyway? She'd call it passion, but those images of women on the covers of novels at grocery checkout lines with their heads thrown back and wearing strategically torn frocks, *burning with passion,* made her sneer. Whatever she'd lost didn't feel *cheap.* And it wasn't like the three-hundred-dollar calfskin gloves she couldn't find;

she could buy another pair at Saks. Purchasing power and shopping venues were not solutions. Her best friend Clara, who had never been married, said she didn't know what Vicki had to complain about: regular sex, someone to go camping with or to the movies, someone who liked her, someone who was dependable and affectionate. She said, "Vicki, this isn't stock trading. Fact: the older women get, the less viable a commodity we are in the commercial enterprise of relationships. You think you can find someone better than Greg?"

Not better, different.

Was Vicki going to ruin a perfectly good life by indulging in some throwback, adolescent restlessness? Clara didn't believe that either the problem or the answer was with men. Vicki almost agreed, but nobody liked to think of herself as the problem. It was nicer to think that men were the problem, or American culture.

Greg and Vicki owned a Victorian in the Upper Haight that had gold-toned hardwood floors lit with spears and chunks of light from the windows, and antique furniture from his grandparents. It was full of funky art and knick-knacks that someone else dusted. Vicki worked as an economic consultant for a big firm downtown. She hadn't had affairs. She didn't think she was going to get what she thought she wanted from one of them instead of from Greg. But how much easier this whole thing, whatever *this* was, would be if she did think that. She used to be one of those people who always knew what they wanted. And now?

A plague of restlessness. So she had agreed to come to Tashkent and talk about private property, what it was and why the government might want it and how they might get it going. She felt like a champion of American values: own yourself, own your life, own your destiny and fate. Begin with your apartment. A colleague's wife, who was from Tashkent, had set Vicki up with Olga and Misha. The idea was: wouldn't it be nice to get to know some locals and the culture from the inside out? She hadn't expected people whose main concerns were how much she'd eaten and how much things cost. They sighed over Brezhnev and sausages. Yet who was she to criticize? Sausages, rent, love: weren't they equally essential? Perhaps her expectations of the world were askew.

One day Olga asked Vicki if she thought they could come to America, and Vicki tried to picture Olga shopping at the Marina Safeway in San Francisco, infuriated that people spoke only English. Some people could not communicate without language. Misha fired rapid Russian at Vicki, his hands useless in his lap, then walked away in frustration and disgust when she didn't understand a word. She wanted to coach him, tell him to slow down, use simple words, use gestures. How would they function in America? She felt her heart rate increasing just thinking about those two: Olga and Misha. They had taken her over, like a foreign infection.

When Vicki was almost finished with breakfast, Misha came back into the kitchen, coughing, and started chopping carrots, potatoes, and beets. She knew what he'd done: Vicki had opened the window in her bedroom a crack because it was overheated and stuffy; Misha had closed it with a bang. He yelled at Vicki for not eating enough, for not making her tea strong enough, for wanting to go out alone without an escort. It was so ridiculous she almost laughed. She wanted to put her head down on the kitchen table in surrender. They win. She was twelve years old, maybe sixteen. How did their son cope with this treatment? Perhaps it was a question of perspective; Misha wasn't yelling—only providing information. This wasn't anger—Olga and Misha simply had loud voices. But in Vicki's family, with her parents, this would be yelling and she would be in trouble. She was surprised she remembered what it felt like to be in that kind of trouble. She smiled at Misha and said nothing. These were her problems, not theirs.

Olga took Vicki to the local militia office to register as a foreign visitor. They waited an hour in cold sunshine for the office to open while Olga chatted with the others. Vicki could tell she was clever because she made everyone laugh. She had a sharp tongue, a watchful eye. At the same time, she was powerfully dolorous. Whenever Vicki asked how she was, Olga said *plocha,* which meant "bad," and she said it like she was dying. Olga always behaved as if nobody would help her with anything, but when Vicki offered, Olga looked as if she wanted to belt her in the chops. Olga was short and wide, built like a chest of drawers. She buttoned her coat all the way to the top, wore her fur hat firmly over her ears. Her gestures had the force of a dictatorship. She was a bulldozer, a hacksaw, a large and sharpened set of pruning shears.

Another hour passed once the doors opened, and Vicki began to feel guilty that Olga was taking time off work. Vicki wasn't accustomed to the bureaucratic meanderings of the former Soviet Union. Olga, unperturbed by the long wait, borrowed a pair of reading glasses from a bulky woman with football shoulders to fill out a form. Then she asked Vicki for dollars, holding her hand out impatiently. *Shit.* Vicki had asked Olga before they left the apartment if she should bring dollars. She thought Olga had said no, so now she had no dollars. Perhaps Olga had thought Vicki was asking if *she* had dollars. But of course Vicki knew Olga didn't. In the militia office, surrounded by Uzbeks and Russians, everyone in voluminous coats, caps and fur hats in hand, Olga was disgusted with Vicki. Vicki was stricken and felt that she had failed a significant test. In Olga's mind Vicki had just proven herself incapable of going to a foreign country alone to provide economic advice. But it was an honest misunderstanding, and Vicki didn't think it was just cause for chewing her out in public. Not that anybody else was paying attention. In the end, it didn't matter. Olga went to work. Vicki returned to the apartment to fetch cash for the registration fee, relieved to be alone, taking buses and the subway, wandering among solemn-faced people wearing dark clothes. She met a man who gave her a subway token. Bogdan's father was Ukrainian, his mother Uzbeki, and he was suave and handsome, offering to buy Vicki coffee at the Hotel Uzbekistan. Was he being polite to a foreigner? Was he trying to get hard cash off her? Was he trying to pick her up? She looked him right in the eyes and couldn't tell what kind of invitation it was, but she got a hot feeling anyway. He said, "Life has changed here," sighing heavily. "Lenin used to stand in the central square. Now there is a globe." He dropped his eyes and might have been looking at her chest. The subway stations were Tashkent's beauty feature, but Vicki was distracted. What was the allure of morose men? Bogdan told her about his life: his first wife was Russian and he had a blond, blue-eyed son; his second wife was Tartar and he had a black-haired, brown-eyed son. Then he talked about his Pakistani business partner who had a wife and children in Pakistan, a wife and children in France, and a girlfriend in Tashkent, and who recently fell on some ice, injuring his back, and now couldn't work and was going broke. Maybe Vicki was wrong about affairs; they seemed to work for others, or at least they provided distraction. In the sway of the subway, their shoulders touched. *We're both married,* she told herself. Besides, she had to deal with the militia registration responsibly or Olga would probably have her arrested. And also, nothing had happened except an invitation for coffee. Vicki wondered what the Russian word for *infidelity* was. Fact: plenty of people were restless.

She politely declined Bogdan's invitation for coffee and got off at her stop to change to a bus. On the bus, a man shouted in her ear, and she finally realized he was trying to ask for directions. She told him she didn't understand Russian. The man looked startled and upset, as if people who didn't speak Russian had no business on his bus route. Did she belong here or was she an outsider? Even she felt confused.

At the apartment, Misha yelled at her even though he didn't know what had happened. When she returned to the militia office, the officials greeted her like an old friend. They drank tea and chatted in the back room despite the lack of a common language. She collapsed into the hard-backed chair, as if it were comfortable.

Afterward, she went to the Museum of Fine Arts, with its flaking walls and badly hung exhibits, the paintings crooked and the lighting dim. But there were beautiful, intricate Uzbeki rugs in patterns of dark design and delicate gold jewelry. She was the only visitor and wandered through the cold rooms, listening to the soft echo of her footsteps. She stopped in front of a contemporary abstract painting, bright swirls of paint like moving bodies. She thought about her sex life, which didn't resemble the painting. It was more like a regular exercise program: a brief warm-up (foreplay), segue into aerobics, gradually building (in and out) heart rates, which was maintained for a while before speeding up and finishing; bingo, she and her husband could eat an extra piece of toast if they desired. She didn't want a *healthy* sex life. She had no problem resisting anything that was healthy. She wanted decadence, irresistibility. She caught herself glaring resentfully at the painting.

Walking away from the museum, she imagined the former Soviet Union spreading around her, from the Bering Sea to Poland. It was just as she thought it would be, bleak and winter-bare, stoic people standing in lines to buy loaves of bread and skinny, half-plucked chickens. *Tashkent* and *depressing* were like *California* and *liberal,* a matched set: buildings were stocky and stiffly blocked; streets were eerily vacant; cars belched black exhaust and stuttered in an aged, decrepit manner; everyone's expressions revealed permanent lines of disappointment; fashion was tasteless, anti-fashion. She felt chaos lurking, invisible—shut in, shut down. A shop had two tubes of toothpaste and three packs of gum under a glass counter, one giant-sized bra and one shirt hanging from the ceiling, and on a shelf, a jar of preserved pears, worm holes showing black as bullet entries.

Olga came home from work, her hip hurting, her face sour. The doctor had examined her and her blood pressure was 220 over 120, so she was ordered to stay home. Vicki rubbed the tension in her forehead; they were both going to die while she was staying with them. Misha yelled at Vicki for going onto the porch. Apparently it was too cold to step out for a minute. She came right back in, nervous about upsetting them further. They watched the most popular TV show in Tashkent, a soap opera from Mexico, dubbed in Russian. Fernando was scheming for Maria, who was in love with Juan Carlos, who was semiconscious (did that mean he was conscious only when he wanted to be?) in the hospital. Olga and Misha argued about the price of sausages.

They stopped talking at the sound of a key in the door. Then their son was in the hallway, stripping off his coat, hat, and scarf. Olga and Misha became festive, and Vicki realized that Anton was the doted-upon household pet. He was tall and pale with a prominent, curved nose, a full mouth, and abundant dark hair. They were crammed in the hall, just outside the toilet, and for a moment it was like a bad cocktail party. Anton was attractive, but Vicki didn't like the feel of his thick, damp hand. They moved into the living room, and everyone talked while Vicki watched the soap opera. She was glad Anton had come, in case one of his parents had an attack. Then he said to Vicki, "You are staying in my room." With his high school medals and yellowed homework assignments pinned to the bulletin board.

"I hope you don't mind," she said. He was a psychiatrist, younger than Vicki, though she couldn't tell by how much. She couldn't remember if he had a girlfriend or wife or neither.

"My parents say you will work here."

She nodded. "I'm going to advise the government about private property." She didn't want to talk to him, felt cheated that he was the only person who had arrived in the apartment who could speak English. Was there no one else? The man in the downstairs hall who watched her like a Soviet spy when she left or entered the building? Maybe he wanted to speak English, but maybe he knew she was a capitalist infiltrator.

"Come, let me show you some things in my room."

What?

Vicki followed, looking over her shoulder at Olga and Misha, glued to the television. The first time they had been silent. She had an itchy, suspicious feeling. Something was about to happen, and it was out of her control.

Anton directed her to the bed and shut the door. Vicki sat with a sigh. Everyone in Tashkent treated her like she could be ordered around; she succumbed. Misha had closed the window, so the room was stiflingly hot. Anton pulled a photo album from a bookshelf and sat beside her, bouncing the bed. This mattress of his wet dreams, of adolescent masturbations and sexual fantasies. He opened the album across her knees and began a tedious recital of each photo. They were terrible photos; the people distant and out of focus, in murky light. She was quickly bored by the meaningless recitation of names. It was like the book of Genesis: "This is Arsen, son of Nellie and Vadya. Here is Irina and Tanya, daughters of Frieda." And so on. He was leaning close, his leg along the length of hers, and she tried to sidle away. His breath was sweet. She thought she might gag. Not since high school had she been stuck in a room with a person of the opposite sex, parents lurking behind a closed door. Then she felt his hand on her thigh. She lifted the photo album and removed it. He smiled happily. "I've never had a sister," he said, bouncing the bed some more. Regression was a contagion in that apartment.

"What do you mean? If you had a sister, you'd try to seduce her in your room?"

"No. Of course not. I like the idea of you sleeping in my bed."

What kind of a psychiatrist was this guy?

Anton stared at her. "You are very beautiful, but not like a Russian girl at all."

That was ridiculous. She was not a girl and she was not beautiful; she was completely ordinary but she had a substantial chest, and that meant some men never saw the rest of her. Vicki took their attention for what it was: love of large tits. She didn't tell him she was married. She was having a hard time believing she was older than sixteen. She stared back at him as if she'd turned to stone. He leaned over and kissed her. She was not stone. She kissed him back. He skillfully—not at all like a high school boy—laid her back onto the bed, untucked her shirt, and slid his hand up her ribs. She wanted to laugh because she was making out with Olga and Misha's son in his room, in their apartment while they watched TV on the other side of a wall. But he was getting her attention because he knew how to kiss. He deftly unhooked her bra, lifted her shirt. He was working fast, using both hands, licking her neck. She tried to wiggle into a more comfortable position against him. She was completely wet and realized this hadn't happened to her in a long time; she'd been sleeping with the same man for fifteen years in undisturbed privacy. They heard the telephone ring, followed by the ever-mournful voice of Olga. Anton bolted up and yanked Vicki to a sitting position. Misha opened the door. The phone was for Vicki.

"Victoria Shepard? This is Mikhail Yevshenko, your interpreter."

"Please call me Vicki." She noticed that Anton had Misha's nose, only Misha's had collapsed into a soft bulb.

"I would like to arrange to pick you up tomorrow evening."

She felt her bra bunched up near her collarbone and her wet underwear.

"Okay." Pick her up? She wasn't scheduled to begin work for three days.

"There's a dinner for consultants at the Hotel Uzbekistan. Do you know it?"

His voice was marbly, rolling with a pleasantly deep thrum. She nodded into the phone.

"I can come to your apartment at five o'clock and we will go in my car, yes?"

"Yes," she said obediently. He gave her his phone number in case she had questions, and they hung up.

She sat back in the chair. Anton was staring at her chest, dazed. She felt hollow, like some bottom had fallen away. Had Olga and Misha told him she was married? She didn't care. He spoke to them, then said, "Follow me." They returned to his room.

"Don't they wonder what's going on in here? I'm going to get in trouble," she said, and her heart started to beat hard enough for her to feel it.

"I told them you want to talk in English without TV sound. Quick, we have little time."

"Wait. A condom?"

He nodded briskly, opened a desk drawer and rummaged in the back, pulling out a wrinkled packet.

Was she going to trust an old, communist condom? "Lock the door," she commanded. She thought they should do it properly, clothes off, on the bed. But Anton treated their previous stint as sufficient foreplay and came at her like she was his calisthenics drill partner; the bed squeaked and her head kept banging against the bookshelf. She dried up and arrived at that brutal moment in sex with a stranger —which she remembered from pre-Greg days—where she just wanted it to be finished, but she had to wait until the guy came. She had never figured out how to say, time's up, bud, remove the equipment. She hadn't expected to need that skill after meeting Greg. How much she took for granted about her life.

In the other room, Misha started coughing, and she listened carefully for his ragged inhaling. The phone rang and Anton paused, but Olga's conversation was seamless. Slumped in their chairs, how well could they hear? It was about ninety degrees, and Anton was sweating onto her. She wondered what Soviet sex education had been like. Maybe there was no Russian word for *clitoris,* which might explain why he hadn't touched hers. Adultery was so easy, she was surprised she felt neither remorse nor satisfaction. In fact, she felt nothing. Like eating a quart of ice cream when you're depressed: a physical activity that had no real bearing on the core problem and left you fat, which only made things worse.

He came, kneaded her breasts in an idle, friendly way, and stood up. She closed her eyes because she didn't want to see a strange, naked man putting on his clothes. He left the room. She dressed, ran a comb through her hair, picked up a packet of photos. With Greg on their front porch. They weren't sitting close, but his arm was around her shoulders, slung like a rope between them. Love: watery and polite, sweet and placid. She felt irritated.

A knock on the door. Anton was smiling in the hallway; Misha looked suicidally morose, Olga furious. The moment was lost on Vicki; was it because she didn't understand the culture? Or she didn't understand this family? Would Olga yell at her later? She almost looked forward to it.

Anton said he was going to come again the next night, and Vicki pretended that might be nice. "But I'm being taken by my interpreter to a dinner." It occurred to her that she could stay at the hotel. "And there are some meetings I'll have to go to, so I'll stay at the Hotel Uzbekistan." She would call Mikhail to arrange it. *I'm leaving, I'm leaving!* She could jump up and down at the idea of getting out of the apartment.

"Oh." He looked unhappy. "My parents know?"

Know what? That she just fucked their son? That she was leaving the next day? After five days in their house, she knew what Olga and Misha disapproved of and what they thought she should eat and how she should dress, but what they *knew?* Anton talked to his parents in Russian. Olga was angry.

"What time will the interpreter come for you?" Anton asked.

"I'm meeting him by the globe in the central square at four o'clock." A spontaneous lie that gave her a flash of pleasure.

The translation of this information evoked a volley of vitriol from Olga.

"My mother says they should come for you here."

"It's already arranged," Vicki said wearily, though now that she'd lied, she'd have to arrange it herself. "It's okay, I can get there easily on my own." She knew that Olga's real complaint wasn't with the people who were picking Vicki up, but with Vicki for not insisting they pick her up at the apartment, and if Olga knew Vicki had lied, her anger would kill her. Now Vicki hated the lie. She was behaving like the adolescent they imagined her to be, and even the protuberant knuckles of her clenched hands looked loathsome. Probably she would never really mature.

"But your luggage."

"I don't have very much." She was tired of the conversation. "Good-bye, Anton. It was nice to meet you." She held out her hand to shake his.

He took her hand in a close, warm grip. "Maybe I will see you later."

God no. "Yes, maybe."

On her way to the toilet in the middle of the night, she ran into Olga. Vicki wanted to tell her that Anton was nothing to her, nothing to rave about either, but that wasn't quite accurate. Besides, Olga's wide, puffy face was broken up with bitterness and disappointment, so clear in the half-light of the hallway. Vicki had a moment, dark and empty, where Olga's expression was as familiar to her as her own. She had expected her life to be different. For the first time, when Olga looked at Vicki, it had nothing to do with Vicki. It was just Olga herself, her life coming through her eyes. And she was quiet.

Vicki put her naked butt on the seat where Olga's had just been. The pink walls were water-stained brown. It was so cold she shivered. She looked down at her feet, which seemed foreign to her. Who was this person? She made herself answer the question: *a human being,* she began. She stared at her feet, unexpectedly haunting, long bony toes, the cold room bringing out the blue under the nails. The same blue of the veins beneath the skin of her forearm. *I am a person,* she said, *trying to see herself in a crowd of strangers, speaking a foreign language. I am a wife who has just committed adultery for the first time. I am a woman who does not recognize her own blue feet when they are placed before her in a faraway place.* She yanked the chain to flush the toilet, and the water sucked down like a powerful ocean tide pulling into the center of the earth.

Ugly Man Turning into the Setting Sun

FUCK, CHINA WAS UNCOMFORTABLE. On the bus, he shifted in his seat, which resembled that of a toilet. This was the second and last day of this ride: Urümqi to Gulja. Scenes of San Francisco pushed at him: the hallucinatory hint of salt air, concrete sidewalks, precipitous hills. China, he reminded himself, was out the window. Herds of thin-ribbed horses; stark, wrinkled mountains—not a benevolent landscape.

Martin paid attention to the passing landscape only at the beginning of a bus ride. The morning's potential photos: a man with his pants rolled above his knees driving a herd of goats; long threads of noodles swaying in a disturbingly sensuous way on racks beside the road; a squatting woman over a flowered enamel basin washing her hair; a passing bus with a lone sheep balanced precariously on the roof.

But without actually taking the photos, he couldn't concentrate, and the disappearing scenes mesmerized him. The morning became a nauseous fog rolling over desolate land; they were moving west. He closed his eyes, head upright, careful to avoid the oily stain on his seat back. Hangover: what was morning without that? He succumbed to his thoughts and was felled by the hatchet of the past. The last time he'd made love with Sharon. Well, attempted to. Ice-blue sheets, pink light from the bedside lamp, the curve of her back, which had once aroused him and now reminded him of the shape of a beer glass. Making love to his wife had once been one of the top three things that made his life worthwhile. He stroked the warm skin of her waist. Her flat voice reached him over the cliff of her body. "What's the point?" His wife: blunt, capable, funny. He expected a witty, sarcastic comment to follow, but there was silence, and he realized she was holding her breath as he smoothed his hand down her hip and thigh. He'd been neglecting her. Finally, with the energy of resignation, she rolled over, put her tongue in his mouth and athletically gripped his hips with her legs. He was surprised by her strength; she'd changed, had been working out or something, and he hadn't noticed. Her body was flexible and springy, with bony shoulder and hip points where there used to be the forgiveness of soft flesh. He knew then that he should stop, that it was going to be like playing basketball on a team with superior players who would be disappointed in his performance. Sharon was focused and hungry. Martin slipped into an abstract dreaminess, prolonging the moment of necessary action, his fingers working while his mind floated away. The truth was, he had no interest in winning the game, no interest in the game at all, and Sharon was right: what was the point? She was wet; he was parched, longing for the liquid release delivered by drink. He didn't know which had come first: drinking followed by sexual disinterest or sexual disinterest followed by drinking. Sharon had turned on her side and slept, apparently without anxiety. Maybe she was satisfied to be right, or maybe she was already planning to leave him, or maybe she had a lover. He'd gotten up, mixed a tall gin and tonic, and watched a documentary about climbing Mt. Everest, amazed by what a human body could choose to endure: unimaginable levels of discomfort, suffering, and pain.

Or there was the scene with Frederick and Margaret, his two law partners, when they'd told him he had to take time off. The evening sun turned Frederick's desk into a black mirror; Margaret crossed and recrossed her legs. "A treatment program," Frederick said. "Three months," Margaret said. "Six if you need it." Frederick straightened a stack of papers, proof of Martin's poor performance. "Not up to par," he said. Martin couldn't remember how he had felt. These were the scenes that lay in his mind, a terrain less appealing than anything he might actually see.

He drank from his silver hip flask. He could spend more money and buy imported gin, but he'd decided to do the local thing. Beers were good, if weak. He was drinking *baijiu,* which tasted like it could strip paint, or the lining of his veins and stomach; pulverize his liver. He was starting to like it. With *baijiu,* there was no doubt you were drinking alcohol, imbibing inebriation. Fuck treatment centers. He'd bought a one-way ticket to Hong Kong and decided, at age forty, to be aimless. He began with China because he knew nothing about it, because the language was impossible, and because it was big. He was going to sink into Asia. Disappear. Fuck them. He pared his life down to a small backpack and his camera. He stroked the hard, slightly bumpy surface of the Leica: compact, light, silent. The perfect traveling companion. Elegant and simple: a 50 millimeter lens—the closest to what the human eye sees—on a Leica body; a stealth camera. Its virtue was that you could photograph people and they never knew, the click subdued, discreet. He was shooting black and white, like a photographer, not a tourist; Cartier-Bresson in China. The feel of it in his hands was as reassuring as a full wallet; it was money in the bank, joy on the horizon. The little black Leica was armor; he could see the world through its dark hole. Words were finally incidental.

They stopped in a village for an early morning break. Passengers trudged behind crumbling mud walls to the row of holes that were the toilets, following the raw, close-your-throat smell of sewage. He left his pack on the bus, taking the Leica in one hand and slipping his flask into a shirt pocket. Everyone left possessions on buses, and Martin had gradually allowed himself to trust his fellow passengers, to follow their example.

He squatted on a log in the pinched shade of a tea cart, sweat slipping down his neck. It was not even eight and already the heat was punishing. Weather as penance. He swigged from the flask and put himself behind the Leica. Blistered air; land like a shed snake skin. He shifted right and found the driver, a tall thick-featured man with rumpled hair and sullen mouth, smoking and talking with his assistant. Driver, assistant, and Martin were all hungover. They had shared platters of gristly meat and slippery vegetables and alternated shots of *baijiu* with bottles of beer. Drunk, it hadn't mattered that they couldn't understand each other's languages. His camera and alcohol—these were the things that freed him from the communication imperative. He was sick of talk, of argument. It seemed irrelevant that Martin knew little of what went on around him in China. He inhaled silence, let his brain swirl with unreleased words. It felt good. Simple as that.

It was the assistant Martin photographed. He didn't look Chinese, with a conspicuous nose, prognathous jaw, and peach pit–sized lumps covering his face and hands. Surprisingly, his limpid eyes seemed innocently unaware of his ugliness. His fingernails were the most arresting: black appendages that grew straight up, perpendicular to his fingers. Were they painful? They were long, too thick to cut. A saw might do it, but no ordinary scissors or clippers. What was it like to have two profoundly ugly physical features? Martin gloated for a moment; he was proud of his thick hair, not even receding, only slightly gray. He had pouches beneath his eyes and a paunch, but he didn't look like a freak.

Nothing about China frightened him. Not the staring, not the incomprehensible language, not the spitting, not the food. The weirder it was, the more he liked being there. It was the perfect place to photograph. Every day he saw things he couldn't have imagined, like the basket of skinned rabbits on the back of a motorcycle. Each fleshy pink butt and stiff set of legs artfully arranged around the edges of the basket, short, skinned tails bouncing, like a synchronized swimming routine. He forgot about himself in the angles of a shot, between light and shadow. The scenes on the other side of his lens swallowed the pettiness of his life, each click a brief moment of release.

Did he like China or hate it? There was the unforgettable day he rode a rented bicycle around Chengdu from one market to another. The photos he'd taken: a man gutting eels as casually as shucking corn, impaling each head on a nail and in two smooth strokes running a knife through its length. He sat in a pool of blood, hands covered with it. The violence, the domestic quality of the scene, haunted Martin. And delicate wooden birdcages with miniature blue and white porcelain water jars. Hundreds of ducks with their feet tied together lying in great placid clumps, stupidly relaxed. It had gone on and on, and he'd felt as if he'd found what he didn't even know he'd come for: the experience of difference. He snapped photos that day the way he consumed alcohol: slaking a thirst. He didn't understand what he was seeing, what it meant, but what was important was the pressure of his eye against the uneven surface of the world.

At other times he hated China for its obtuseness, for the way it reluctantly relinquished its treasures. Parsimonious, that's what this country was. He drank and snapped photos of the assistant and other passengers, strangers he felt close to after a day and night locked in travel with them. They were his leap of faith.

He felt, as he looked at his fellow passengers through the viewfinder, that he knew them, that he even belonged here with them. A warming sensation, separate from the heat of the day and the burn of alcohol, filled him. Nobody would believe that he could feel at home, at ease in such a foreign place, among people he didn't technically understand. He was moving through the world at the beating center of human life. He loved these passengers, this bus ride, this landscape.

Unfortunately, travel hadn't turned out to be the best method to escape thinking. There was too much dead time, too much time in which all that could happen was contemplation. The problem, he dimly felt, was that each memory hit the same note and he couldn't see it in a different way. Sharon had moved out a month before

Frederick and Margaret had given him the boot. "I'm tired of the bullshit," she'd said in what seemed to Martin a feeble complaint. There was something pathetically generic about his life: forty years old, wife gone, job on the line. What do they call it? Emotional bankruptcy. He was a walking therapy case, except he refused to indulge in that self-serving crap. He had just been in a run of bad luck. This was a no-fault situation. He wasn't at fault and neither were they. *They.* He had periodic abrupt realizations: he was alone in the world. This thrilled him—he could do whatever he wanted—and depressed him—nobody cared. He was nearing the end of his first two months of travel, nearing the border with Kyrgyzstan. Crossing a border implied change: a new country, language, life. At the least, plenty of Russian vodka.

They drove on, through swollen hills the color of bones bleached beneath shadowless light. His seat partner had a thug's face, his history visible in the pitted cheeks, the mean plug of a nose. He shelled sunflower seeds, then, to Martin's horror, fell asleep against his shoulder. Martin gently pushed him away, tilting his greasy head against the windowpane. His back throbbed. He inhaled the stink and yellow haze of cigarette smoke, imagining he was in a bar. The man across the aisle smoked incessantly, sunk into his dirty jacket like he had stomach pains; the couple behind him shifted seats to take turns being sick out the window. The impenetrable din of conversation dwindled as people fell asleep. Against the wide, desolate land, the bus full of strangers felt cozy. He slowly twisted the cap off his flask, lingering with anticipation. Then, he drained it. He noted his panic, checked his watch. Ten. The Chinese ate every meal early, but still lunch wouldn't be for another hour. He was out of alcohol; there was nothing left to do except sleep. No need to panic.

He dreamt: letters lay like gutted fish on a glass table

beside cold drinks, the silvery flash of ice, the distinctive scent of gin; letters from a woman he didn't know but desired with the slap of lust. Then he was in the hotel, with shattered bottles crunching underfoot in the hallway and the gray, ruined room with lacy, shredded window screens and spotted mattress. Then, the warm slide of night, moonless, light of diamond-cut stars, a sorrowful "Ave Maria" playing from a fuzzy tape deck somewhere, the crack of an argument in Mandarin, the syncopated loneliness of a dog barking.

Waking, he was lost in the fleeting absence of memory. He had been dreaming of his room the previous night. He looked around the bus and thought, *I have no business here*. A throbbing set up behind his eyes, nose, bony slab of forehead. The bus felt stifling, full of unpleasant smells and ugly people. Maybe he missed Flip, his squash partner. Maybe not.

The bus pulled into a town, the tarmac so hot it swished as if covered in a hallucination of rain. Couples strolled amidst honking horns, blasting trucks, dust, and exhaust fumes as if they were on a tree-lined parkway. Romance seemed laughable in this shriveled land. He thought about Sharon but couldn't imagine kissing or holding her, maybe ever again. He quickly shoved his pack into the seat corner. He had to buy booze. One thing about China: if you were a man, you could do what you wanted and nobody thought anything of it. You could drink beer at seven AM; you could buy liquor before eleven; you could dump your girlfriend off the back of your bicycle if she was annoying you. Anything. The shop had one plank shelf with a single line of dusty bottles. He bought a liter and didn't prolong the pleasure, just opened it and raised it to his lips. He leaned against the outside wall and let the liquid slug down his throat.

Back on the bus, he picked up his pack and sat with it in his lap. The confusion of reboarding, passengers resettling and rearranging. The zipper wasn't closed all the way, the heft and balance different. He unzipped the main compartment. The Leica wasn't there. His heart clenched. He felt around inside. Perhaps he had, in his I-love-the-world moment, dropped the camera into the mess of clothing. He came up with his bag of film. Relief at having his film flushed through him, but the loss of the camera! Stupid, careless; he should never have left it, even though everybody else seemed to leave things on the bus. Moving through the world without the Leica was like traveling naked. Being naked was for showers and sex, and he certainly had few opportunities for the former and no interest in the latter. He pulled himself together: someone on the bus had stolen it. The driver and assistant had been within sight of the bus the entire time; no stranger could have boarded. They were nowhere. What was the thief planning to do with the camera? Who would understand its beauty?

He began in the front row: the Üighur woman he'd snapped pulling folded bills from the top of her stockings at the afternoon stop yesterday. She lifted her dress, cocked her knee, and bent her kerchiefed head. Her legs were surprisingly well-shaped, hidden beneath a boxy, flowered dress. Then the three men he'd caught drinking jars of tea and eating hard-boiled eggs in a shred of pale shade, together but separate, not acknowledging each other. He had been absorbed by the angles of their bodies, the geometry of human clusters. There was the woman who looked like a whore, in her shiny wine-colored dress stretched tight over the loose flesh of her belly, whom he'd caught with a snarl of boredom on her face. And an old man with a bristly gray head, a worn gold band on one crooked, spotted finger. His expression was beyond calm, as if "outcome" were not a concept he bothered about. Martin had examined each of them through his viewfinder; they seemed familiar.

All those photos in the absent camera. And the photo of the two men across from him, leaning forward in their seats and dropping spittle onto the floor, their defining gesture. The photo of his own seat partner as he'd shoveled noodles into his mouth, his chin bowl-level. Pretentious to consider himself an artist, but the photos were his work. Really he knew nothing, hadn't seen enough, didn't know what to look for.

Do something. He wove his way to the front, gripping seat backs for balance. He was surprised how much he understood. He understood the assistant's grave face when Martin showed him the backpack and mimed a camera and then made a gesture that combined flying and grabbing. The assistant conferred with the driver and they motioned Martin to return to his seat. *Now what?* Returning to his seat, Martin looked into people's faces. They didn't look back. Perhaps everyone was in on it. An anti-foreigner act—not a conspiracy exactly; that sounded too paranoid. Just a perpetrator plus accomplices, an action with consensus. He wanted the thief caught, punished, full of regret. It was probably a man, and Martin pictured him with his head bent forward, hands cuffed behind his back, contrite. Martin would take a photo.

It was late afternoon when the driver pulled off the road beside an aqua lake and a poor, flesh-toned village. Whitecaps chopped the water, cut by a hard, dusty wind. On the far side of the lake, green grassland unrolled into meadows, pine forests, snow-lined peaks. A man wheeled his horse to a stop in a cloud of dust and leaned toward the driver through the window. The bus doors remained closed, the engine idled. Martin poured the remainder of the liter of *baijiu* into his flask with shaking hands.

No explanation was provided and the passengers sat quietly. They knew something, or they knew not to be inquisitive. Two policemen wearing ill-fitting, olive-colored uniforms arrived. They looked through people's possessions, working methodically down the aisle. Windows were closed to keep dust from blowing into the calmed bus. The driver turned off the engine. Martin swallowed from his flask. He was surprised by a lurking sense of guilt. Was he the cause of this? But stealing was wrong; he wanted his camera. The thief deserved punishment. People were careful to keep their eyes on the floor, the lake, their own laps. An unspoken rule: when there was trouble, you looked away. The old man, peacefully waiting for the bus to move, was the only unruffled person. The bus stank of cigarettes and fear. The policemen searched Martin's pack, examining his bag of film as if it might have the camera hidden in it.

It happened quickly. The thief was a man near the back Martin hadn't noticed. The tall policeman handcuffed the thief's hands behind his back and pushed him down the aisle and off the bus, just as Martin had imagined. Except the thief held his head up, not proudly, but with an angle of doom, and his body seemed to shrink within his clothing. The face of the thief was not memorable—Martin would never have taken his photo. The short policeman carried Martin's camera. Martin wanted to grab it from him, prevent it from being dropped.

They forced the thief to kneel in the dirt a few yards away, facing the lake, the wind flapping his jacket like bird wings. The passengers stood to watch, crammed in a clammy lump on one side of the bus. The only passenger who didn't stand was the old man. Nobody was shy about observing whatever was going to happen next. Martin stood at the back, taller than the others, capable of seeing without touching anyone else. What *could* happen beside this lake in the middle of nowhere? The only sound was the thick voice of the wind. And him. Martin heard himself as if the interior of his body were hooked up to a microphone. The steady whoosh of blood pushing around miles of tubes, slap and gurgle of liquid in his stomach, pulsing bass ache of his back muscles. The tall policeman drew a pistol, placed it against the back of the thief's neck, forcing the man to drop chin to chest. The policeman pulled the trigger. The thief fell forward.

Martin buckled his knees, sat back in his seat. He felt strangled, choked. The noise of himself grew, filled him. His brain had snapped a photo of the thief on his knees in the dust, the gun stuck into his hair, the slump of his body. From perpetrator to victim, just like that. Martin felt frantic. He had imagined the thief in handcuffs, contrite, no more.

The bus changed, swollen with voices and a ponderous silence. The short policeman stood above him, holding out the Leica. Martin hung the camera around his neck, something he never did because he didn't like to be obtrusive. More than a camera now, the black box felt cold and heavy against his chest. He huddled in his seat like a naughty child, unable to look at anyone. *Escape.* Shouldering his backpack, he rose and took himself, his camera, his guilt, his booze off the bus. It surprised him that nobody tried to detain him. He was the victim of a crime; he was an accomplice to a murder.

Heavy gusts of warm wind pushed him toward the lake, and he walked unevenly, his hair shearing sideways, his T-shirt sailing away from his body. He didn't know what he would do or where he was, and a spasm of uncontrolled exhilaration made him flap his arms. He was drifting loose. The setting sun slanted across the empty land, relentlessly luminous. The world was beyond his capacity to understand, vibrating around him in a thrilling disturbance.

The assistant with the black fingernails ran after him, shouting. Martin turned, lifted the Leica to his eye, and looked through the viewfinder. Everything from the fluttering grasses at his feet to infinity was clear within the frame. The cool, indifferent box in his palm, the smooth movements of the lens between his fingers as he turned it to focus. What kind of act was it to use this instrument that had caused the death of a man? Anarchy, rebellion, callousness. But his stomach was full of churnings, and his veins pulsed. He set the assistant's face in the central rectangle, slowly focused, drawing the face toward him, and snapped the man waving his hideous hands. At the last minute, the assistant flinched, turning his head so the lumps on his face were silhouetted against the background: the parked bus, a dusty hill, a crystalline sky. Ugly man turning into the setting sun.

Norris

NORRIS PUT ON A PAIR OF SWEATPANTS
and socks beneath her hospital gown.
Warmed with anticipatory pleasure, she
bent slowly to fit her heels into her shoes
and tie them. Then she had to sit down on
the edge of the bed. Lying flat on her back
she felt nauseated, but in a vertical position the nausea was dramatic and she felt
as if she were falling from a great height.
All it took for life to seem dangerous was
a change of position.

The door to her room was slightly ajar,
and she kept her eye on the opening; either Artemis, her primary care nurse, was
going to walk through, or Betsy, today's
nurse, who would then probably ask why

Norris was getting dressed as if she were going out. She thought about what she would tell Betsy: *I just wanted to wear street clothes before I died.* Or, *I'm tired of my butt flapping bare naked in this half robe.* She could say she was cold. Then her temperature would be taken and probably some more blood drawn and God knew what other tests performed in a ridiculous attempt to discover why she was cold and what this meant about her condition. She was dying—that's what everything meant. Except she wasn't cold, she reminded herself, eyes still on the door, so it didn't mean anything except that she was lying.

She didn't quite believe she'd managed to persuade Artemis to do this; and now either he was twenty minutes late or he wasn't coming. He had argued that his job was on the line, that he couldn't take a patient out of the hospital without a doctor's order. With his beautifully shaped head, long, graceful cheeks, and smooth black skin, he was the most soothing person Norris had ever looked at. More than six feet of unruffled calm. She found no edge to grasp, no way to make him do what she wanted.

The previous midnight he'd stood, big hands spread around narrow hips, elbows in the air. "Whooee. Ms. I-Travel-the-World-Alone can't go out alone. Who else on this planet seen you beg like this? I bet never outside a bedroom."

"Nobody as beautiful as you. Anyway, we're in a bedroom. More or less." The hospital was in a state of hushed silence that implied rest, but the staff marched the hallways briskly, and Norris knew that most patients, like herself, were kept awake out of pain, restlessness, or boredom.

He sighed. "Girl, you've been able to get men your whole life to do what you want. Even without your hair, and skinny as a sick goat, you look good. But I don't care about your looks. I like you, but I'm not taking you outside on my day off. You're here because you're sick; you need to be in here. The end."

She laughed, but it was more like choking and her eyes watered. She reached out and touched a tattoo on the inside of his left bicep, running her finger over the soft skin where there was a small blue-black heart with HIV+ in the middle and an arrow halfway through. "Artemis, you know better."

"Yeah, okay," he said. There followed a long silence in which she felt frantically unable to determine what decision Artemis would make. As a way of preempting disappointment—an underrated emotion—she forced herself to abandon hope of escaping the hospital. When he finally said, "Tomorrow, at 11:00, after rounds," her whole body quivered as if she were coming down from some high.

Now, thirty minutes after he'd said he'd come, Artemis's long black fingers gripped the door's edge, pushed at it. "How are you, darling? Give Artemis one of your pretty smiles." He was his usual exuberant self, except for his lowered voice, to avoid attention.

"You're late."

"Aren't we friendly today?"

"Fuck off."

"Uh-huh. It's a damn good thing I like you bald and sullen, girl."

He pushed a few buttons on the IV machine, stuck a thermometer in her mouth, and held her wrist, counting her pulse. His black fingers made her skin look inhumanly pale.

"Can't we just go?" she mouthed around the sheathed, plastic stick beneath her tongue.

"You're lucky to have me, girl. Best nurse on the floor, with a little *Saturday Night Live* thrown in. It's my Jupiterian side makes me appealing. Plus, I'm handsome, smart, know how to cook a steak, and can speak French.

Not to mention the fact that ain't no one else 'round here put up with your foul mouth or take you on an illegal outing." He ran a hand softly through the few hairs left on her head. "My Norris. You've got a nice-shaped head."

"Shut up about my bald head, Mr. Jupiter. Let's go."

"You ate lunch today, didn't you? Barbecued chicken? Worst you ever ate? You must be feeling fine if you're eating." He checked her temperature.

"Feeling fine is no longer in my repertoire."

Artemis rolled his eyes. "Don't be losing your humor on me, getting like Madeline."

"How's she doing?"

He shrugged. "Still alive, not very happy about it."

"Why fight it? Death can't be as bad as dying." Norris never intended to die in a hospital in her hometown.

"Take these." He handed her three pills, different shapes and colors.

"Are these going to make me feel better or worse? Sleepy or wired?"

He shook his head. "Always suspicious. Better."

She put the pills on her tongue, accepted the plastic cup of water he held out, and swallowed.

He pulled a heparin lock from his pocket, unhooked her IV, and attached the hep lock. Next came a pale-blue, long-sleeved cotton shirt from a shopping bag full of clothes. He lifted her arms one by one and worked them into the sleeves as if she were a helpless baby. His swiftness and expertise embarrassed her even though Artemis had seen her body in every soul-demoralizing condition Norris never imagined she would be in, especially before a witness. He buttoned and rolled the cuffs so they covered her hospital identification bracelet. He hitched up the collar and buttoned the shirt at the neck to hide the temporary catheter—for the chemo—at her clavicle. In the same efficient manner, he maneuvered her into a bulky sweater. She felt like a mannequin and wondered how he'd gotten so adept at dressing other people. But the question and ensuing conversation seemed more effort than they were worth. She'd begun to reject whole imagined conversations out of a kind of fatigue that was nothing like not having enough sleep or working too hard. She knew, without anyone telling her, that it was the fatigue of her body gradually shutting down—not for the night, but forever. The last thing out of the bag was a knit cap, which he fitted delicately over her balding head. They'd had arguments about her refusal to get a wig. She was repulsed by the idea of beautifying death, but he said she just wanted to offend everyone who came to see her with the awfulness of her condition. Her body stood thinly in the clothes, like a solitary blade of grass. "I look wretched," Norris said to the mirror over the sink.

"Yes, ma'am, you look mighty sick."

They slipped out of her room and strolled down the hallway, conspicuous in their innocence. Norris looked into rooms. She saw flesh-colored, praying hands holding a spray of stiff yellow carnations on a bedside table beside a mauve, kidney-shaped plastic basin. "Death is tasteless," she said.

"Just like daytime TV." Artemis led her into the service elevator and inserted a key into a notch so the elevator couldn't be stopped.

"You're perfect," she said.

They took back hallways, but it was slow. Norris had little strength. Glossy slabs of linoleum stretched into exhausting distances. Artemis held her elbow, his thumb firm against bone. "You eat your Wheaties this morning or what? We got to speed up, Norris. Half this hospital knows me, and they see me walking out in street clothes with a corpse-thin woman, we're in trouble."

They went out a service entrance used by employees for smoking. The unfiltered sun made Norris's eyes water. Artemis pulled out two pairs of sunglasses and gave her one. She was used to the lightness of her hospital gown and felt burdened by the heavy clothes and tennis shoes. "I look like a drug addict."

"Ooh, you are skinny, girl."

Around the corner, Artemis checked the street traffic and said, "Looks cool. Where to, my Norris?"

She felt giddy with the delight of having gotten herself out of the hospital. Departures always gave her a sense of accomplishment and of impending surprise. "The beach."

He looked skeptical.

"We'll walk to the park, then get a cab. Do you have money? I'll pay you back."

"Sure I got money. You're my date."

At the corner, Norris stopped, breathing heavily. Her lungs felt shrunken, too small to take in the amount of air she needed. Cars sped past, jockeying for position, leaving the stinging smell of exhaust. People pushed around her, running for buses with bulky shopping bags in their hands. Faces were tight and empty. Norris imagined their problems: credit card debt, a daughter on drugs, someone dying of cancer in the hospital. A piece of Janey's advice popped into her mind: when you walk around, make lists of things you have to look forward to so you won't develop frown wrinkles. But it was hard to think about the future so specifically, and wrinkles didn't matter to her. In the noise and bustle she felt unpleasantly querulous and trembly, filled with a disappointment as poisonous as her illness. Her delight faded; San Francisco gave her no sense of elation. She understood all the bits of passing conversations, could read all the signs, knew the parking regulations, recognized the fruits and vegetables in the market, could imagine details of the lives around her.

"I can't make it to the park." Norris sounded pathetic even to herself.

Artemis waved a cab down. The driver had a hooked nose, skin the color of bark, with a black mustache dense as a small animal on his upper lip. He had an accent. Norris leaned forward. "Where're you from?" she asked.

"Pakistan."

She sighed audibly. "Which city?"

"Peshawar."

"Ahh, lovely." The driver's name was Shahid and he said he missed the mountains north of Peshawar. Norris had been there twenty years before, arriving about six months after she'd left San Francisco—her original departure. A beautiful Afghani man had gotten her high on hash, and she'd walked through the old city surrounded by fierce men in turbans and by blue-eyed water buffalo. She'd seen plastic balloons, one in the shape of a pink elephant, another a Santa Claus complete with insipid smile, and never knew if it was her imagination or reality. She remembered the hotel she had lived in off Grand Trunk Road, and the lecherous, old mercenary who had taught her the proper way to drink Russian vodka and then how to throw a knife into the pillows on his bed at Dean's Hotel. She started to cry. Her hand was enclosed in Artemis's, resting on his thigh as if they were lovers. Her knees were sharp, pointing nowhere. Tears moved down her cheeks; she felt as if her chest would crack.

"Go into the park down South Drive, toward the beach to that lake on the left," Artemis told the driver. Then to Norris, "Girl, forget about the world—you've seen all you need of it, more than that." He pulled a bandanna out of his pocket, lifted her sunglasses, and wiped at her cheeks. She kept crying. "Going somewhere makes me happy, the one sure thing." It hurt to cry, her bones and muscles aching terribly.

"Maybe. My theory is you been moving around trying to keep your troubles away. But, girl, trouble travels free of charge. I moved cross-country and for three whole weeks felt like I'd escaped. Then the same problems moved in and lay down underneath my bed like smelly dogs."

"Yeah, you work around dying people, people with worse trouble than you've got," Norris said with sudden energy.

Artemis laughed.

"I can't die here," she said.

"That's the stupidest thing I ever heard. Course you can die here. It's no different from anyplace else: human beings, piece of ocean and land, troubles, good food. You just learn what it is to settle in and be at ease."

They stopped at Mallard Lake. "Getting out?" the driver asked.

"Let's sit here a minute and then go to the beach."

When the driver rolled his window down and wrapped his arms around the steering wheel, Artemis opened his door to stretch his legs. Norris looked at the lake, an arrow-shaped pool of brown water overlaid with a glittering, gray film of light. All the trees had lost their leaves and were as naked as her head in the sunshine. She imagined herself walking around the edge, through the wetness of soggy leaves, the feel of the grass, mud close to the water. But she couldn't move. Ducks paddled around, occasionally diving in nose first.

As a child, she had often tried to get her parents and sisters to go bike riding in Golden Gate Park, but nobody ever wanted to go. How had this place lost its power to thrill? She left San Francisco when she was twenty-five years old, after her grandparents died, leaving her with an inheritance, and she stayed away twenty years. She stayed away because she'd made a life for herself, a life of moving around between unfamiliar places, and because the longer she was away, the more impossible it became for her to imagine a life in one place as sufficient. She required the unfamiliar the way most people required the familiar.

Now, away from that free reign of restlessness, the past twenty years appeared in her memory as clips of images pinned to a series of hotels, rented rooms, or apartments, and the people she'd lived, eaten, and traveled with. She'd seen little of her family and had stopped missing them long ago. It appeared mutual because they hardly wrote. Once, when Norris was in Chile, her mother had sent a family photo to the Poste Restante in Temuco. She'd examined the photo on the trip back into the mountains, squashed between sheep and farmers and a couple of cases of beer in the open bed of a truck, gusts of cold air slapping at her cheeks. The family, minus Norris, was arranged up the grand sweep of staircase in the entryway of her parents' house overlooking the bay. There were her two older sisters, Melina and Evan, their husbands, and five children of varying ages. Norris knew a couple of the children by name, but not all. Everyone stood stiffly in sharp, shiny clothing, their smiles cracking across unblemished, carefully bland faces. Their clothing, the way they held their bodies, the slender climb of the staircase, the extravagant, carved banister and flippant curve all looked preposterous. She had thought how unnecessary everything in the photo seemed, how inessential to life. Norris recognized her mother's handwriting on the envelope, but there was no letter enclosed, not even a note. It was as if the photo had been sent to signal her final exclusion from this family. She didn't blame them. She'd excluded herself, though out of indifference, not anger. The people in her family were no more special to her than anyone else she might meet and come to love somewhere in the world. She didn't subscribe to the idea that there was a finite limit to the number of close relationships she could have. There were hundreds of people capable of being sisters to her, or parents, friends, lovers. It wasn't that she didn't miss people—she did. But she would meet others. Over and over again she created intimate connections with people, and then left them. She liked the freshness of encounters; she had developed a callus over the sadness of leave-taking.

Despite opportunities, she had never married or had children. Leaning against Artemis in the taxi, a soft, dreamy sadness filled her, a delicious regret. The way she sometimes felt about missing the events of her generation: Woodstock, the Vietnam War protests, the Summer of Love. It wasn't real regret, only regret that she created to intensify her own experiences: Afghanistan before the Russians came; living against a glacier in Chile; the edge of civil war in Sudan. Even after all these years, when she set out for an unfamiliar country or town, her heart rushed as though she were in love. Alone in the world, she could meet anyone, do anything, and go anywhere she wanted. Her time belonged to no one and nothing else. Her life seemed without end, a single line before her, devoid of obligations or the weight of responsibility to mark it, to puncture the seamless stretch of time. With that kind of life, it was impossible to anticipate death in any profound sense; there was no routine, nothing deadening in it. The world was too big, too present for her to consider her own dismissal from it as anything but insignificant. She hadn't been useless; she'd volunteered in refugee camps around the world, taught English, worked in health clinics. She'd taught herself to knit and draw, speak eight languages well, many others well enough. The world was her most constant companion.

"You ever been to Egypt?" she asked Artemis.

"No. Doesn't seem like the right place for a big black man. Besides, it's a hungry country and I don't like to be hungry."

"Lots of beautiful men there," she said.

"I'm not a slut, Norris."

She nodded. Artemis might prefer the Seychelles. She had been in the Seychelles when she finally recognized she was ill. Carlo, the Italian she'd been traveling with for nearly a year, had just left to visit his mother back in Italy.

Norris stayed on in their rented one-room hut, close to the beach, with a deck all the way around. She turned forty-five. Her surfboard was propped against the wall while she swung in a hammock, wrapped in a shawl despite the steamy weather. Next door was a young English couple: the woman in a string bikini and the man with three earrings in one ear and the right half of his head shaved.

Janey came over one afternoon, sat on the steps, set a beer on the deck planks, and lit a cigarette, her fingers stacked with silver rings. "Where'd your husband go? He shouldn't have left. You don't look good."

Norris had no idea how she looked: long hair in a loose knot on top of her head, no jewelry, a pair of baggy shorts and a boxy T-shirt. "I don't have a husband."

"How smart of you." Janey dragged on her cigarette. "Mine's a headache. Marriage is disappointing, or maybe men are. I can't tell anymore if it's him or the institution.

All he cares about is rock 'n' roll and looking at other women. He's a musician, so he gets to do a lot of looking anyway. I'm used to him, though." She waved her cigarette in the air. "How do you give things up? I don't even know how to give this up."

Janey started coming over every day, fixing Norris's hair, bringing food, and talking through the blue-shadowed afternoons. Her voice was pleasant and she made herself laugh a lot. She gave Norris advice about what to use on her face to keep her skin from drying and about how she should call Carlo and have him come back. Norris liked Janey, her casual assumption of care.

"Norris, you're sick and you should go home," Janey announced one afternoon.

Home? She had herself, her few possessions, her collection of strangers.

"It's been a long time," Norris said.

"So?"

She looked down at her legs. They were flat and thin, the muscles depleted. She hadn't even walked to the beach since Carlo left, much less surfed. She hadn't eaten more than toast and pineapple. Suddenly she felt how weak she had become and how far she had deluded herself into thinking this was a temporary illness. She decided to go back to San Francisco; maybe she would recover there.

And now she was stuck in a hospital in her hometown, not getting better. The worst kind of death. She had made a will fifteen years earlier, requesting that her body not be returned to the US if she died abroad; she should be disposed of the way the locals were wherever she happened to die: buried, dropped into the sea, burnt, left to the birds. It didn't matter. Now she would have to be buried or cremated in America. It made her restless to contemplate; it erased the life she'd created. Unrequited restlessness.

"Let's go," she said to Artemis and the driver.
They drove to the beach and down the Great Highway
toward the zoo. Air blasted through her open window.
She loved it: the slight stickiness of salt, the impact of
moving air. At Taraval, Shahid pulled into a parking lot.
Before they walked off, he whispered to Artemis, "Your
girlfriend, she is okay? I can help?"
Artemis shook his head. "Just wait for us."
Norris took off her shoes. Water filled the view—big,
gray water. She inhaled the smell of salt, set her eyes on
the line where water met the sky, imagined herself on a
boat rolling the edge of the horizon away. Waves broke
steadily against the sand in a white, frothing line stretching the length of the beach. Wind and water, everything
seemed to shift and bob. She walked toward the horizon,
the world floating away from her, out of reach. "I used to
imagine scenarios for my death, unusual stuff. Maybe
killed by random gunfire in a Mafia shoot-out in Catania,
Sicily. Or drowned in the Ili river when my jeep rolled off
the side of the Tianshan Mountains in northwestern
China." She paused. "Did you grow up near water?"
"Plenty water 'round New Orleans, but we hardly left
the city. My grandma and her sister and my mama, and
all my siblings, we just stayed in the city. It was us and the
steps to our building and the street. Course, then I did
leave." His voice was sad.
Norris paused and knelt down to put her head between
her knees.
"You nauseous?"
"Yes, sir."
"We should be heading back anyway."
"I feel bad, Artemis. Is this all it takes to die—pain,
discomfort, nausea?" It was nothing like a hard trip. There
was no sense of going anywhere, no anticipation of un-

known pleasures waiting in another place or at a later time. And all she thought about was herself, her pain, her sickness. Cancer of the self. "How did you think you would die?"

"Well, I never thought about disease, even after nursing school. Always felt too healthy and I feel good now, so it's easy to forget. Too easy. Most days I can't feel it. Why I got that tattoo. Well, that and my sick humor."

"I guess I could be thinking about what I haven't done in my life, but nothing comes to mind. Shit, I feel so lousy I don't even want to talk about food or sex. How pathetic."

They strolled without speaking, the only sound Norris's breathing. "You know, people have these lives where they say they never *did* anything. I wonder what those lives are like." She was out of breath, air wheezing up through her lungs. "I thought I'd never regret anything, not what I did or what I didn't do." Death was full of regret.

She sat down, put her head between her legs. "Maybe your life always looks puny in retrospect." The sound of moving water filled her ears, as if she had gone deaf to everything but the ocean. She remembered a song from her childhood, an inane, soothing tune: *I am a bubble. Make me the sea, make me the sea, make me the sea.*

Artemis talked to her. She watched his mouth, the large, graceful curve of lips. She let herself sink into the surging sound of waves. Traveling had taught her to wait, to accept flawed bureaucratic systems, to embrace inefficiency, mistakes, malfunctions. She had become generous toward the world. Once, beside a beach in Cuba, while waiting for a bus that never came, a woman holding a broken-armed umbrella had said, "If you can't *be* still, you can still your mind." They had been talking about the woman's children, about marriage and money, and the statement had come as a surprise, and Norris had remembered it and repeated it often to herself: *A still mind, if not a still life.* A man from Peshawar waited in a car. She wouldn't go back to that hospital room. She wouldn't die in her hometown.

"We're going back to your room, Ms. Sickly."

"Why are you named Artemis?"

"I thought it would tame my testosterone, to have a woman's name." He laughed. "It didn't really work, but I like it anyway."

Norris sank into the backseat of the cab, exhausted. The seat was lumpy with parts that poked her bottom and this cheered her, the discomfort of travel. She asked Shahid, "Do you miss Peshawar?"

"Yes, ma'am."

"Your family's there?"

Shahid talked to his wife for ten minutes once a week.

"Artemis, let's find a travel agency. I want to buy Shahid a plane ticket to Peshawar." The passing landscape out the window spun too fast. She leaned back, closed her eyes, and handed Artemis her credit card. "Let's go buy airplane tickets." She felt light, that rush of anticipatory pleasure over a journey.

Artemis wiped sweat from her temples and put an arm around her. "You sure you want to do this? You going to be all right?"

"Yes. And I want to buy you a ticket somewhere. Anywhere you want."

They stopped at a travel agency on Irving Street, and Norris slept in the back of the taxi, lulled by the sounds of traffic and people speaking Russian, Polish, and Chinese. Artemis brought her a cup of water. "Okay, girl, come and sign." They entered with their arms linked. Shahid stood stiffly, tense with excitement.

The travel agent, a blond-haired man named Kevin

Fletcher, pulled up the tickets. "Shahid's flying to Peshawar for three weeks."

Shahid bobbed his upper body in a cluster of small bows. "Thank you. I am very happy, very lucky. Thank you."

"I'm going to New Orleans," Artemis said. "To see my family."

"But Jamaica, Borneo, Madagascar? You could take a friend."

"Someday." He winked at Kevin, who blinked his pale eyes rapidly. Shahid went outside to smoke a cigarette.

"Artemis, there's nothing like going some place unfamiliar. Please, buy another ticket." She was almost crying. "It's important, you don't know. You could take one trip, not forever."

"Me and Shahid, we just want to go home, girl. New Orleans is warm, and I can eat crawfish, oysters and crabs, my grandma's succotash."

"No," she said.

"Look, going away isn't always about going someplace strange, you know."

Norris shook her head. "It *is*. That's the whole point; you go away to a place you've never been before. There is no exhilaration like it."

They stood facing each other, a long-married couple carrying on an old argument.

Artemis turned, put his hands on the desk, leaned toward Kevin. "Where would you go, Kevin?"

He rolled his chair in retreat and coughed. "Depends. For museums and sophistication, London, Paris, or New York. For the slow life, the San Blas Islands off the coast of Panama. For the exotic, I'd try the Antarctic."

Norris stared at him, as if mesmerized by the ships on his tie. "Can you arrange for me to get to San Blas?" Norris said.

"You can't go," Artemis said.

"Somebody has to go someplace interesting."

"I'll lose my job. What if they find out I took you outside the hospital?" Artemis waved his arms.

"They won't find out. I'll discharge myself against doctor's orders."

"You die out there, you're leaving somebody a big hassle to get you back and bury you," Artemis said.

"I arranged for that a long time ago."

Artemis turned to Kevin. "You can't sell her a plane ticket. She's got cancer."

"I'll go by ship," Norris said.

"Look, Norris, the pain is going to get worse, and then what're you going to do?"

"At least I'll be happy in a foreign place, surrounded by strange—"

"What makes you think you can get to Panama by yourself?"

She thought for a minute. "Some strength kicks in when I'm alone. The energy of anticipation."

Artemis sat heavily in a chair. "Nobody *wants* to die alone in a foreign country."

"It's not like anybody is going to die *with* me."

A cover of silence, a sheet drawn over a stilled face.

"There are always memories," Kevin suggested softly.

"Memories are consolation prizes for losers," Norris said, and the silence that followed was bitter and weary.

"It's over, honey. Cry if you need to," Artemis said. Norris didn't look at him. She couldn't respect him for choosing, out of the wide world, his hometown.

She was in her room on the eighth floor with the familiar view of steam pouring from a vent below, a concrete building, and a few spiked green treetops. She knew the sun was setting, because the column of steam turned golden, slashed with pink and gray. She remembered more spectacular sunsets: quick, heartbreaking equatorial bursts of light in the Galapagos Islands; desert skies streaked in a long agony of color in the Sahara. Being in a hospital was like being on a very long flight: no stops, no fresh air, no sense of day or night or reality. She'd tolerated those flights for the end results, though she preferred the pleasures and inconveniences of overland travel. Here, too, she awaited the end result.

"How're you doing?" Artemis reattached her IV, helped her undress, and get into bed.

"Fabulous."

"Sarcasm isn't always an attractive quality, you know." He squeezed and massaged her shoulder before rubbing an alcohol swab in a circle against her skin.

"Fuck attractive qualities."

In fact, she felt terrible, nauseated and trembly, defeated and sad. One of her oncologists said the cancer probably began three years before. Conceived in Uganda, gestated in Kenya, Tanzania, Madagascar, the Seychelles. Born in San Francisco. In Uganda there were pink flowers big as mutant melons blooming along the walls of buildings, and views of misty, densely forested hills. She was aware of death there, where the locals called AIDS "the skinny." In large numbers, death looked small; only now that death was hers did she appreciate its size. All that she had done, might yet have done, falling away from her, forming dense, lovely piles of experiences, places, encounters around her. The piles grew larger: what had been her life peeling away and lying about like useless material. She sat up for a moment, just to feel the flutter of physical sensation that small movement gave her. Then she lay down, feeling herself falling, falling into a still life.

Mapping the River

The Waiting Room

ANNETTE RAISED HER EYES, BUT THE two hundred people staring at her did not flinch or look away. It was their steadfastness, a staggering absence of self-consciousness that awed and deflated her. She was in the waiting room at Shiliupu Wharf in Shanghai, and she believed she had a ticket to Chongqing, on a boat up the Yangtze River. In fact, she didn't know what she held in her hand: a small rectangle of cardboard printed with characters, none of which matched the ones she'd found for Chongqing, no numbers, no time, no date. She wasn't sure how much she'd paid for it, and when she remembered purchasing it—standing in the wrong lines, people pressed up against her back impatient with her fumblings—she felt triumphant that she'd walked away with something and ashamed at being so ignorant of the language, the rules, the patterns of life in China. Through much effort, she'd discovered that the boat left at noon. She inhaled and exhaled, nudging at the plug of nausea that occupied her center. The air smelled of garlic, pickled duck eggs, cabbage, cooking oil, and something metallic, industrial. A pungent, slightly sour effect—a burnt sensation in the back of the throat. It had been twenty years since she'd traveled like this—one small pack, no reservations—and it made her aware of how ordinary and stable her life was; being loose in the world was disorienting.

The wharf waiting room: large and gray, icy air blowing through broken windows, long benches filled with people and their mounds of belongings, mangled sounds of conversations and crying children rising into the high ceilings. She crossed and uncrossed her legs, shifted her weight against the hardness of her slice of bench, and took shallow breaths. She hadn't settled onto real ground since she'd left San Francisco for Hong Kong, then Shanghai, ten days before.

She had forgotten how to wait, how to let time settle like a fine dust. She wanted to do something; she wanted action, but she forced herself to sit still, her eyes straight ahead, focusing on nothing. Perhaps her stillness would divert the starers. Groups of people roamed the waiting room, walked down her aisle and stopped in clusters to gaze at her. The excruciating sensation of exposure. The cloak of language difference was like gossamer, not a shield at all, more alluring than pure nakedness. She noticed, out of the corners of her eyes, that many people were actually openmouthed in astonishment. What could be astonishing about her? Slight build, short, thin brown hair, green eyes, and pale skin. Her skin: that random arrangement of soft dents along her cheekbones, across her chin, as if someone had tossed pebbles into the pond of her face. But she wore makeup, so a person had to be close in order to see these marks clearly. She could have had surgery to erase them, but for her they were a talisman from the bottom of her life. At 11:00 the doors opened and the mass of people trampled their way to the exit, shoving onto the boat. Crushed like a walnut, she was squeezed out of the waiting room.

The Boat

From the corner of a bench on a lower deck, she watched as the boat pulled away through clots of rusting, decrepit ships, bottles, plastic wrappers, and Styrofoam lunch boxes floating on the oil-slicked water. Cigarette butts and the hulls of sunflower seeds already littered the deck. A young boy swung on a gate and threw some wadded paper over the side. Thrilled when it was thrown back, he cast it again and again into the arms of the wind. Energetic conversations in Mandarin camouflaged an emotional, almost-familiar ballad blaring over the PA system. She didn't feel excited about this journey, but rather ill at ease. She had decided that a one-way ticket across the globe was a good way to break from Eric; she needed the refreshing blast of travel to foreign places. Refreshing. She had thought China would be exotic and wonderful, and she had wanted to see the Yangtze River gorges before the Chinese government built a dam and their beauty was underwater forever. But so far, China felt like a cheerless, neglected room full of excessive numbers of people with bad breath.

"You speak English?" A small, pale man with thick glasses close against his eyes sat down. "First time in China? Tourist or work?"

"Yes, a tourist." She spoke slowly, careful not to slur words together.

"You are married?"

"No."

"How old are you?"

"Thirty-six." She had no reason to lie, but it gave her a jolt, a sense of being on the run.

"Oh." Thin hands held in his lap, he looked away from her, thoughtful. "But, children?"

Fuck. She hated strangers who asked probing questions. Why not just ask if she'd ever had her heart cut out, pounded with a sledgehammer, then buried? She took a deep breath of her own soured, familiar rage. "No." A word awash in guilt and sadness. She said nothing of the child she was tentatively gestating. An obtuse gesture: to travel to a remote country, pregnant, without even speaking the language. A pregnancy she could barely admit to herself, much less anyone else.

He looked sympathetic. "Where do you live?"

Back into innocuous territory. "San Francisco. Do you know it?" She felt an urge to giggle; she sounded like a foreign-language tape, bright voice, each word dropped like a single colorful crystal.

"Oh, yes. A Chinese man made the bridge, the Gold Bridge. Very beautiful."

The Golden Gate Bridge made by a Chinese? Designed or built? She knew nothing about the bridge. Surely Chinese people knew all the important details about famous structures in China. "You live in Shanghai?" she asked.

"My family is from Nantong. My parents live in Ürümqi. I go to school in Shanghai. I am going to visit my grandmother in Nantong."

"And Chinese people—are happy?" How shallow and inane this notion sounded, spoken to a stranger in another culture. Maybe no one in China cared about happiness, maybe they cared about socialism. She and her friend Pearl had been discussing the slippery qualities of happiness for years; were they happy? Was it a respectable goal?

He folded one beige, polyester-clad leg over the other and smoothed the sleeves of his brown sweater. "China is changing. It is slow, but better. Deng Xiao Ping is a great man. He has made mistakes." He paused and let his crossed leg swing like a pendulum. He wasn't wearing as many clothes as she was, but perhaps he was used to the rawness of the weather. "Now the Communist Party is careful, after the events in the spring of 1989. The older people and even middle-aged people, they like this government. Life is better."

"What is your job?" she asked, automatically keeping the conversation afloat.

"I'm studying in university for a doctor of solid mechanics. These birds here," he pointed to the seagulls flying in the wake of the boat, "they are there because of solid mechanics. The boat moves and there is air and it makes it very pleasant for them to fly." He paused and watched the birds, mesmerized. He seemed so spare in his appearance, without any excess. She liked the pure, translucent cast to his skin.

The crowd around them moved closer as if they wanted to embrace her, staring, lured by the alien sounds of English. She wondered if the solid mechanic's habit of looking straight ahead, as if he were talking to the birds, was his tactic for dealing with the crowd, looking through the people as if they didn't exist. They blocked her view, made her feel breathless and impatient; she wanted to sweep them off the deck, hear the splash and clatter of their disappearance into the river. She was cold, turned heavy and dull by the slow, stilted conversation. It felt hard to lift herself through the words. She left, as if fleeing persecutors.

The Cabin

She awoke from an afternoon nap to the sound of someone hacking violently and, through a slit of velvet curtain, saw a man spitting over the railing into the river.

Her cabin was on the top deck with two beds, a dirty slab of red carpet, a sink, and a cracked mirror. A window with a red star in the middle of it and maroon velvet curtains faced the river. The pillows on the bed were covered with flowered towels instead of pillow cases. There was a dusting of cigarette ash, like individual flakes of snow that never melted, on the carpet beneath the bed. It was all slightly repellent. She sat up, swung her legs to the floor, and felt so dizzy she put her head between her knees. She had only eaten two oranges all day. Her body had that unmistakable feeling of being an inhabited space. She crouched on the edge of the bed, her chest flattened against her thighs, still with her fear, a fear that felt personal, as if it had been waiting for her. She held her mind tightly, like a bug enclosed in her fist. She couldn't look at what it would mean to have or not have this child; love was dangerous and stupid.

She found a small deck around the corner from her cabin at the bow of the boat and sat on a coil of rope. The long afternoons of China: sticks of bamboo poking out of the water, signaling what? Three lumpy hills like mutant breasts in the distance, and packs of smokestacks running amok along the skyline. It was an uninspiring landscape, bland, gray, slightly out of focus. This was not what people traveled for, such paltry surroundings. There was something liberating and intimidating in the unattractiveness. She was a flawed tourist in an imperfect place. There was no pressure to have a fabulous time, to be amazed or riveted by China. But she felt trapped on this boat, with little to absorb her interest; what was she meant to do here?

"Lewis is dead." She often said this flatly to herself, without emotion, as a way of defining the harshness of reality. "My son died when he was four years old." A truth that never left; the one thing that she could never change. What was the word for mothers whose children had died? She was not widowed, which was a possibly elegant state to be in. She was bereft. When he died, Annette understood that pain could not be taken away or shared by anyone; it was a powerfully solitary experience. Her grief had grafted onto her, was a part of who she was: Annette and her grief, Annette and her dead son. When you had a child, it was for your whole life, one way or another. All of the attention, love, time, money she had bestowed on Lewis had failed; a fruitless investment. He was her interrupted creation, forever unfinished. When she thought about his death this way, she felt a disorienting, fierce anger.

She touched her face, smooth pads of her fingertips rubbing the three largest dimples atop the cheekbone beneath her left eye, as if for good luck. A triad of nicks, another cluster of flaws pitting her chin; these were her memory. Alone amongst a billion people, a spasm of restlessness snapped through her. She needed telephone calls to make, social obligations to keep track of, other people's troubles.

She needed somebody or something to dress for. Distractions were what got her through life. She thought about her job as the marketing director for a large cosmetics firm, the crisp morning light through her apartment in North Beach, the garish exuberance of Pearl's laugh, the inside of her own refrigerator: bottles of nail polish and champagne, celery and sticky chunks of Gorgonzola and Brie cheeses. How many days to Chongqing? The abrupt spareness of travel.

The sun set, a simple circle of orange firing the pollutants in the air. The sky bruised into shades of blue and gray as the boat cut through cranes and tankers into Nantong, a town of factories. Seagulls dove for dinner. She thought of Mr. Solid Mechanics getting off the boat and taking a bus to his grandmother's house. She imagined a table filled with bowls of the food his grandmother would have prepared for him, the warm light of the rooms, the heat of being in the presence of those who loved you. She sensed China, its bulk and awkwardness, the weight of its people, all paired or in families, around her like a reproof.

Hunger

In the morning she walked past the second-class cabins: bunks stacked to the ceiling, a haze of laundry lines hung with flowered washcloths and shirts, the floors thick with unimaginable food debris and general detritus. Attendants swept the mess into big dust pans and then tossed it overboard into the flat, wide, essential river. She stared into each smoky doorway. Men and women in pajamas, illicit glimpses of private moments. She felt skittish under the squinting stares that came back at her from beneath sleep-rumpled hair, through the curl of morning cigarette smoke, an intimacy of strangers. Her cabin, by contrast, seemed luxurious and dull.

She didn't know the name of the boat, how many people were on it, where the cafeteria or snack bar was, if there were emergency exits. She felt hungry, taking a perverse satisfaction in the hollow feeling, in the act of depriving herself of something as primary as food. When she got off the river in Chongqing, she would need to know: birth or abortion. There was plenty of time to fly back to San Francisco. Like a string constricting her finger to remind her of something, her reasons for not having another child were obvious. But the string loosened and then she was lost, filled with anxiety and anticipation.

The sounds of the outside lower deck: teeth tearing at sugar cane, sucking inhalations of cigarettes, sunflower seeds splitting. The travel habit of endless snacking. About twenty people stood so close she heard them breathing, smelled the garlic. A harassed father chased his thick-eared son to keep him from flinging himself overboard. A grandmother yelled at her two grandchildren in a shrill voice. The boy cowered and cried, the girl ignored all verbal assaults and placidly fired her plastic submachine gun into the crowd. A baby drooled on Annette's shoulder as he was held aloft while his mother watched Annette write; the miracle of English unfolding across a postcard. Children seemed to be everywhere, even in this country of mandatory birth control.

A man launched into a lecture on the business of exporting concrete. "You must be lonely, not speaking Chinese," he suggested and invited her to Huangshi. "It's a heavily industrialized town, built in the 1950s. Its products include nonferrous metals, iron, steel, et cetera." She almost laughed at these selling points. She itched to roam

her mind undisturbed, though she craved distractions to keep her from her own thoughts.

When she stood, bodies brushed against her and she clenched with claustrophobia, her pool of anger ready to spill. A young man with permed hair and tight silver-studded black pants leaned into her ear. "How old are you?" She stopped, confused. His sultry, lewd tone didn't match the question. The tide of China had moved in, lapping at her feet; how to step out of it when she couldn't see its edges?

She fell onto her bed, the blank, public face of her cabin. It could be anywhere, a room no one cared about. A rectangular piece of river passed across the open door: flat boats with motors that shrieked or groaned, one hauling three dead pigs draped over the bow and a hold full of bony cattle. A woman from the back of a boat dipped a bucket into the river three times, an ablution of dirty water. Hunger, nausea, restlessness cycled through her and, in a stupor of panic-induced lethargy, she let everything pass. After a stop in Nanjing, the banks of the river were green with firs and poplars spraying the skyline. The delicacy, the sudden beauty in the monotonously unattractive landscape, made her heart ache. She remembered a sign in her Shanghai hotel that admonished, "Regain your Vigour in Tourism." She didn't know what day it was, what time it was, when the boat would arrive in Chongqing, what she would do when she arrived in Chongqing, whether or not she was going to have this baby.

Lewis had been an accident. At the age of twenty-nine, she'd gotten pregnant during a brief affair with a man called Chard, short for Richard, though Annette never knew if his nickname signified the vegetable or the condition of being very burnt. He had waist-length dreadlocks

and was from New York City, and by the time she discovered she was pregnant, he was gone. From the moment Lewis appeared—a dark-haired, wild distraction—he'd been more absorbing and entertaining than Chard would ever have been.

Her life had slackened after Lewis died. She lacked sufficient strength to reshape it. Her friends suggested therapy, grief support groups, meditation, even the numbing balm of Sunday mass. But she couldn't focus on her own reformation and she made everyone uncomfortable with her weeping and rages.

There had been men, in clusters and series, but none of them had caused her to feel anything more than the soft zing of sexual attraction, or inappropriate, savage annoyance. And then Eric, ten years younger, the wrong person for her. They shared lust and a disconcerting mixture of incompatibilities. They disagreed about foreign policy, causes of depression in young women, what to eat, whether to go to a movie or a museum on a Sunday afternoon. He was bossy and controlling, yet she persisted with him, with an energetic inertia. Here was someone to fight with, an arena for the anger that turned even her sweat bitter and potent. Their arguments often ended in sex, as if they were acting through the script of a standard relationship. There were nights with him she wanted to see only through the fog of imperfect memory. In her cabin, she examined her damaged face in the cracked mirror: without makeup, beyond the scars, it was obvious she was aging. She hadn't wanted to get pregnant. Certainly Eric lacked interest in fatherhood and neither of them would choose the other as a long-term partner. Still, although she was too fearful to face the jury of her own being, she knew what might satisfy the speechless mess of her insides. Now, she was

pregnant and alone. Which had seemed interesting, even challenging, when she was twenty-nine.

She sat down and ate some crackers she'd bought in Hong Kong, flipping through her phrase book. She practiced the phrase Wo *huai-yun you liu-ge xing-qi le*: "I'm six weeks pregnant." She sighed. It was very slow travel, moving against a river's current.

In Huangshi, two men resembling her grandfather, in caps and V-necked golf-style sweaters, moved into a cabin next to hers. They greeted her in Mandarin, staring openmouthed. She thought her fly was down or she had toothpaste smeared on her face. They talked and laughed and, framed in the square of her window with the red star painted on the glass floating above their heads, flung beer bottles and cigarette butts overboard. Their voices entered her dreams as she slept in the afternoon. When she awoke, she stretched and felt the strange suppleness of time. She could do anything. The total absence of obligation thrilled her and she lay in bed full of nothing.

Late that night, after changing into sweats, she flipped aside the curtain to see the stars. A cheek like the slap of a hand, a blooming nose, an eye huge and distorted, peering in—it was one of the men from the cabin next door pressed against her window, hoping to catch a glimpse of her body. Hasty disappearance. She panicked; what if they tried to break into her room? Ridiculous, on a boat full of people. Her old rage clawed from her belly into her throat; she could scream. She paced her small cabin, glared at the unoccupied bed; if she had a roommate, this wouldn't have happened. But she might have an awful roommate and be grappling with other problems.

Calmed, she slept through the stop in Wuhan. At the edge of dreams, she sensed the boat dock. She wanted to wake up, but couldn't get her eyelids to lift. She thought someone was trying to open her door. She felt sick, fearful, sure that she was going to be attacked in her bed by the men next door. Finally, she lurched from her bed and checked the key. Locked. She lay back on the bed to the sound of her own breathing; she was alone, in the middle of China.

Food

The third day: cool wind, choppy water, haze hiding the banks. They appeared to be crossing a lake. The men next door passed her quickly, heads down. They looked guilty and slightly hungover. She'd eaten all her snacks from Hong Kong, and it was clear she was going to have to eat in the cafeteria. The thought made her queasy with anxiety; buying food in a foreign language with a crowd of people watching. She felt bored, her jaw tight, aching, held like a box sealed off from social interaction. Pale light painted the floor of her cabin from the open door. She put on her sunglasses and stood at the railing outside her cabin. She didn't know where to send her mind; the past was too dark, the future unknown, the present hard to grasp. The intensity of her solitude made her sad, but she didn't want to immerse herself in China; people stared, made her feel alien and more alone.

In the afternoon, Nick, an Australian from Perth, emerged from a cabin two doors down. He'd boarded in Wuhan during the night. He had black, curly hair, blue eyes, and seemed oddly inept—stumbling sentences and fidgeting hands—even while he was physically fit and had an air of practiced charm. He immediately began to talk, leaning beside her on the railing. He told her he'd quit his job as a surveyor and had enough money to travel for two years. He said he spoke fluent Chinese and invited her to dinner in the cafeteria. She was happy to be speaking rapid, fluid English, to be listening to his.

A steamy, crowded, low-ceilinged room. People scrabbling to obtain bowls of unrecognizable food. Large round tables covered with bones, rice grains, spilled beer, splashes of chile sauce. Nick directed her to find seats while he entered the fray for food.

The heat and press of bodies. She sat down at a table with two women drinking beer and spitting fish bones onto the floor. One wore a synthetic white blouse decorated with lace and faux pearls. The other had drawn a mouth different from her own with lipstick, excess lip hidden beneath foundation. They stared at her briefly but were more interested in their own conversation. It made Annette calm to sit beside them; they didn't stare at her. They looked tough, experienced, as if nothing could make them flinch.

"Rot," Nick said and slapped four bowls onto the table, two of rice and two of cabbage and meat. He smiled. "It looks dreadful, doesn't it?" He plowed into the food, shoveling neatly with his chopsticks. "I like the horror of this." He waved his arm, indicating the smoky scene. "I think about the stories I'll tell: the spit, ghastly food, foul smells, crowds and pushing, cigarette smoke, surly officials. The repressed intellectuals, the peasant politics, the suppression of culture, the greed. Great stuff for stories, a little annoying to live through."

"It all sounds exaggerated and improbable." Annette picked carefully through the cabbage, marinated in grease, to avoid the gelatinous white chunks of pork fat in her bowl. She watched him eat without her particularity, the long spread of his hand on the table, the surprising dexterity of his fingers with chopsticks. He seemed enviably adept at coping with China and things Chinese. "How did you learn Chinese?" She was a terrible traveler, absorbed in her own situation more than in China. How small and petty she was; how grand China.

"I started learning Chinese characters when I was fourteen as a kind of game, and then I couldn't stop. It was quite odd to arrive in Beijing and understand everything, even though the way of life is so foreign. I'm glad I came, but I wouldn't say I like it here. What are you doing in China?"

"I came to see the Yangtze River gorges." She couldn't discuss breaking off with a man by going away, or resolving the dilemma of pregnancy. She looked into her bowl of rice, forcing herself to collect small globs of rice between her chopsticks and raise them to her mouth.

Nick was looking at her, awaiting further explanation. She was distracted by the women at the table; they appeared to be trying to listen. Nick didn't know a thing about her. She could define herself to him as she wished and she would never see him again. No one knew her on this boat. No one who did know her knew where she was. She began to talk, but it was the things she left unsaid that sparked through her.

"I'll find some cold beer and let's meet up on the deck, okay?" He stood up to leave and looked down at her. "You have beautiful eyes." His charm seemed to have gained momentum, leaving her with an impression of competence and grace.

He was thirty-three years old. The age she had been when Lewis died. She could drink a beer if she wasn't going to keep this child.

After he left, the woman with the artistic lipstick leaned forward and whispered, "What about sex in your country?"

"What?" Annette asked, suddenly panicked. Had she and Nick had a conversation about sex? The women conferred in Chinese and giggled. Then, a slow whispered sentence: "How not get baby?" Annette looked around, wondering why they were being so furtive. "Most people use condoms; then you don't get sick or have babies." Disease was a better word, but it seemed too advanced. "Have to marry?" Back to slow, careful English. "No, you don't need to marry. Some people think you need to marry, but other people don't. In America, people do what they want." She didn't know if this was true or even if they understood her. It was hard to make generalizations about life in America. She was probably wrong and half-expected to be accused of being a fraud, not a real American.

The two women nodded, talked to each other softly, then: "You are marry?"

"No."

"How old are you?"

"Forty-one."

They actually gasped, covered their mouths. They were much younger and they weren't married. Annette was old, unmarried, pregnant. They told Annette that men in China refused to use condoms, most women were on the pill, and virginity was still important. Their attention shifted to Annette's arms. She'd pushed her sleeves up to her elbows, baring her forearms. Both women stroked the hair, surprised. Annette couldn't move, stunned by the unexpected familiarity of being touched. Then, they left abruptly. She watched them walk away, hips rocking, worn black pumps thwacking the floor. They were likable even if they had been visibly appalled that she was over forty and unmarried, even if they had petted her like a household pet. She looked at the soft, pale hair on her forearm. She had mostly been living in her head and was unbalanced by this flurry of interaction.

She walked slowly back to the upper deck to meet Nick, her mind quivering and shooting around inside her like a nervous grasshopper. The two men in their golf sweaters—were there even golf courses in China?—were doing their usual, leaning against the railing, smoking, drinking, and looking across the river. She felt surprisingly fond of them, of their routines. They were neither completely good nor completely bad. She entered her cabin, shut the door—dark, private, quiet. Her clock ticked softly from the table, a navy blue sweatshirt and a pair of pants on the bed, her toothbrush, tube of paste and comb next to the sink. She looked at the pants and pictured herself too large to fit into them. It was tempting to close the curtain, crawl under the quilt, and lie quiet and still, but she was aware of China, vigorous and waiting on the other side of her cabin door.

The burnt orange ball of sun drifted through a hazy sky, setting fields of golden rapeseed alight. Nick handed Annette a beer as she sat down beside him on the deck. "I thought you weren't coming," he said. The sky turned a fuzzy gray and then, very simply, it was night. The moon hung, black water moved beneath them, stars shone white and still. The boat slugged against the current. The air was damp, a cool hand on her cheeks. She lifted the beer to her lips and paused without swallowing, then secretively poured some out into a coil of rope. She told herself this was not a decision.

"In the old days, men hauled boats up the river against the current. Brutal work." He took her hand, stroked her fingers. "All the things this river has witnessed: hard labor and illness, anger, betrayal, death, birth, love." She pulled her hand gently away. She liked talking to Nick, but she wasn't imagining more with him. Men seemed like insects, essential to the workings of the world, fascinating to watch, sometimes beautiful, and just fine as long as they weren't too close to her.

Land

After days on the boat, she was surprised to be on land, walking the streets of Yichang, lit by a few faint, yellow street lamps and the harsh bare bulbs of food kiosks. She ate squares of tofu with chile sauce, a bowl of noodles and dumplings, powerful flavors, like a punch to the belly. She felt as if she could not eat enough. It was ten o'clock on a Tuesday night. The boat was moored in Yichang until midnight.

She noticed every detail, as if Yichang were under a microscope and she were a scientist looking for the mysteries of life in the slow, enlarged movements under the glass. A market was closing down—cheap watches and pants, stiff bras stacked like piles of gleaming, snow-white funnels. Stern-faced men sat in barbershop chairs under the night sky having their hair coifed by women earnestly blow-drying and applying gel. A shop selling TV repair equipment gathered a crowd watching a soap opera on a small television. At a kiosk, a woman slashed the peel off water chestnuts with a cleaver, then speared them like shishkabobs and set them in a tall glass jar of water; they looked like pale, naked lab specimens preserved in formaldehyde. A man slumped asleep in his cart, his head lolling to one side. A couple rode past on a bike, pedaling lazily through the half-empty streets, the woman humming softly. They moved as if they were savoring the night, their night in their town on a big river in China. What did that couple know of the rest of the world? What did she know of it herself? Their boxed lives weren't even intersecting here, though she could see them and they could see her. She felt a surging fondness for Yichang, each scene a gift of the unknown. She loved being alone and unworthy of notice in that town.

She bought biscuits and oranges from an old man with an unlit cigar between his teeth. She felt her Mandarin was very successful until his wife yelled at her; she wondered what she'd done wrong, stepping back and looking embarrassed. The woman suddenly smiled and handed her a section of sugarcane. Annette looked at the sugarcane, then the woman, mystified; so much could happen between people that was incomprehensible, and yet she knew she'd been given a gift of food. She held the sugarcane in her hand like a passed baton in a relay. Stopping to watch television with the townspeople, she sucked on the sugarcane, spitting the fibers onto the ground just as the Chinese did. She was part of the world, evicted from the cramped space of her own life.

Back on the boat, she left her purchases in her cabin and lay on her back in the dark on the deck, black blanket of night around her, the sound of river water kissing the hull. Were human beings more alike or more different from one culture to another? She felt happy, an unfounded happiness that simply existed and that she knew would go away. She felt its worth, like lotion on the cracked, dried skin of her grief and rage. She fell asleep.

When she awoke, the boat was moving stealthily. She turned on the light in her cabin and sat on the bed. It was 2:30 in the morning; the taste of garlic in her mouth and a musty feeling in her head from waking up in the middle of the night. Still pregnant, still undecided. She stared at the back of her hands, the clarity of etched lines. She felt hopeless and hungry. She opened a packet of biscuits and munched on them; they were powdery and tastelessly sweet.

She spread out the map of China—a bird with heavy wings, awkwardly taking flight. There were thousands of names she could not pronounce turning the hills and valleys gray with print. She traced her way to Chongqing, then let her eyes fall randomly on different names in small and large type: Mianyang, Barkam, Zöigê. Faint pink lines indicated swamp or saline marsh, blue lines for rivers, parallel thin lines for unpaved roads. There were areas without any roads at all. Flat print on paper, that was all it was. A longing filled her, blotchy and borderless, overwhelming. She didn't want it; she only wanted manageable desires: to see behind, beyond the map, to see people riding their bicycles, hear their arguments, smell their cooking. It was three o'clock in the morning and she was moving up a river into the center of China. Maybe all of this movement and everything she saw would make no difference in the end. Like hunger, she would simply be hungry over and over again. She went outside and looked up at the stars, the water passing beneath the boat a soothing sound, like someone trying to lull her to sleep. How could these be the same stars she had looked at her whole life?

The River

Early morning in the gorges: Men poled slim skiffs through glassy, smooth water, cloaked in cool gray mist. The boat's engines were silent and the light splash of water splitting beneath the hull echoed softly against the rock walls. Mountains embraced the river, pressing it into a narrow ribbon. The land was more powerful, larger finally, than the river. Mountains rose from the river's edge and marched backward in ridges of bulky, green-softened peaks. They passed through terraced fields, blooming cherry trees, thick pines with the delicate tracery of trails laced through. The sight of rock walls so close to the boat was startling, as were flashing glimpses of deeply sliced ravines. It was beautiful and Annette had lost any expectation of beauty. Early morning Chopin played over the loudspeaker, a lyrical accompaniment to the hacking and spitting that was the human music of mornings in China. Then the coal town of Badong with blocky concrete highrises set in the midst of deep, pocketed mountains. Men stood in line to carry loads up the hill to the town from barges docked at the river. The day stretched before them, full of heavy labor.

Lewis died in a head-on collision as they were coming home from a party in Tomales Bay. It was December, ten days before Christmas. Her 1968 Peugeot was totaled; she had a face full of glass, a shattered ribcage; and her son was dead. She could hardly breathe, her lungs shrunken and her heart constricted. Blood ran like tears down her cheeks. He had been strapped in according to all the federal safety guidelines; she was technically guiltless. But she was guilty of having a child who could only continually be exposed to danger; she was guilty of putting a child and her own heart into the chilled, indifferent hands of the world.

The driver, a twenty-three-year-old surfer with a blood alcohol level of 1.2, was unscathed. His name was Thomas Harcourt and she remembered him in the circling of red disaster lights, swaying off to one side of their entangled cars, his hands dangling uselessly. He looked stupid and culpable, a hank of hair hanging down his face.

Annette didn't know how he'd managed these last seven years to live his life with the death of a four-year-old in the realm of his responsibility. And she didn't care what trouble this memory caused him.

Banana trees, waterfalls, steep stretches of stained rock, sandy banks and stony beaches, farmhouses with slate tile roofs hidden in the foliage, fields. Once, what she thought were headstones in a cemetery turned out to be rows of plants covered with white cloth. Men fished the river with large, cone-shaped nets. She noticed everything, including herself, in this landscape, legs stretched out on the bow deck across the span of the day.

Nick joined her. "The *Changjiang*—that's what the Yangtze is called in Mandarin— divides China north from south. The houses in the south don't have heaters, houses in the north do," he said. She knew so little about the area she was passing through, facts that could matter. He asked about her travel plans, and she admitted she had none.

"Your job?"

"I've got vacation time built up." Besides, her colleagues were weary of her moods. She paused. "I don't know how it will be to travel pregnant." She was surprised at her decision to have this child, felt a tightening of resistance followed by a strangely, profoundly relaxed moment. Then her nerves began to vibrate and she was filled with the sickening sensation of a person falling in love.

"Ahh." Nick looked thoughtful. "And the father?"

"He's in San Francisco. We aren't involved with each other anymore." She couldn't be sure this was true. The pointless exhilaration of random lies.

Nick looked at her, measuring.

"Where are you going next?" She pulled her knees to her chin, dropped her head, felt ill.

"Bus to Dazu, for the Buddhist caves. Come along."
The river moved steadily, without hesitation or pause.
Having made one decision did not make others easier.
She still didn't know what she wanted to do.

Arrival

At dawn on the last morning, Annette watched a man kill a duck outside his cabin on her deck. He twisted the neck, then sliced it, followed by another twist. Blood drained into the gutter while the duck's feet paddled the air and the thin stream of liquid slowed. He would arrive in Chongqing with a freshly killed duck. His motions were calm, practical, efficient. She thought about a monk she'd watched at a Buddhist temple in Shanghai gravely picking garbage out of a carp pond with a net on a long pole: food wrappers, banana peels, cigarette butts. The Chinese loved throwing things into water. She admired the monk's acceptance. He didn't waste effort on futile attempts to prevent the throwing of trash, signs everyone would ignore. Instead, he simply cleaned up the mess. This was China.

They docked in Chongqing, a hilly city rising steep and gray from the banks of the river. Far away, the middle of China, lettuces drying on lines, old brick buildings dark and closed, a sandy quay, women with clumsy makeup and unfashionably thick stockings under miniskirts, a blind man sweeping a street.

Before the Afterlife

"*Don't say your father and I didn't tell you,*" Mike imitated his mother-in-law, Mrs. Case, in their room at the Hotel Select. "*Go to Hawaii. Now that's a honeymoon.*" Mike sat heavily on one of the narrow twin beds. "Our honeymoon. Separate beds, like we've already been married for decades and romance is gone."

To be fair, Mrs. Case hadn't been the only person to speak out against the choice of Egypt for a honeymoon. Denise's best friend, Cinda, who had been married three times and had a lot of experience with honeymoons, said, "Look, you should go where you can spend most of your time in bed, because that will become rare soon enough.

And when you leave your room, the choices for activities should require no thought and hardly any effort. Real traveling? That's a mistake. Trust me."

But Denise was certain that she and Mike could handle real traveling, even though she had no idea what it was.

Brown stains had turned the green walls of their room fearfully dark. There was cigarette ash along the baseboards and butts underneath the bedside table. The toilets and shower, barely lit and sour with rust, were down the hall. Denise was reluctant to touch anything. But thinking of how appalled her mother would be gave her a way to enjoy the horror. A honeymoon her mother would never take with a man her mother would never have married. Denise felt elated and guilty.

The caliber of the Hotel Select was intentional; Denise wanted to try budget, backpacking travel. "I don't want to be one of those people who go to a third-world country and spend in a day what the average citizen makes in a year," she had said to Mike. "We can be a little uncomfortable; it's not forever."

Denise, who believed in reservations and arriving at airports well in advance of departure times, had planned their itinerary carefully: four days in Cairo, one day by train to Luxor. Four days in Luxor, then two days to travel to the Sinai beaches and a blissful week of relaxation along the shores of the Red Sea, followed by a day of return to Cairo. She allowed two extra days wherever it might be needed; a three-week honeymoon.

They were not efficient tourists. After an arduous trek by public bus, they arrived minutes after the pyramids had closed. They could have spent more money and come on a tour, like sensible tourists. Instead, they faced aggressive camel drivers angling for a final sale, without the buffer of a guide. "Hello, hello. Only ten dollar, ten dollar. Yes, now. Come. See sunset, sunset."

Mike finally shouted, "Go away. We can *see* the fucking sunset."

And they heard a quiet "fuck you" as they trudged across the sand. Mike and Denise exchanged looks. "Exporting the best America has to offer," Mike said. "McDonald's and 'fuck you.'" He looked chagrined.

"What do they expect? They're harassing us. They should be kept under control, not allowed to harangue tourists." Denise felt a moment of dislike for herself. Her tone and her attitude. Who did she think she was, anyway?

They studied the stone structures shaped like corrugated cardboard triangles. "They look exactly like the National Geographic photos," Mike said, disappointed. "You expect something you've traveled halfway around the world to see in the flesh to be *better* than the photos, not equal."

Real life and replicas in a general confusion. How would they know if they were seeing the real Egypt? "'They were ancient even to Herodotus in 450 B.C.,'" Denise quoted their guidebook. "'They are probably some of the oldest man-made structures on earth.'" She had a moment of regard for their age, their long history, the suggestion of wisdom, the things they'd stood silent witness to: plagues, for example, or sound and light shows.

Mike whistled. "Some old shit." He bounced on his toes, pleased. "You won't find this in Hawaii." He put his arms around her—the warm, damp clasp of love. "My brilliant wife. I'm glad you brought us here."

Cairo was heat and noise, the color of bleached ash and hot sand, the air full of exhaust fumes and dust, the streets crammed with old cars, stinking buses, donkey carts, bicycles, motorcycles; the honking a relentless aural assault. Mike said, "If they followed some simple traffic rules, they wouldn't have to lay on their horns like a few million psycho-kids."

"'Cairo has been the largest city in Africa since the Mongols laid waste to Baghdad in 1258,'" Denise read from the guidebook.

"The Mongols were in Baghdad?" Mike asked. "Maybe the world has always been a small place."

They breathed as shallowly as possible—first because the air smelled of broken sewer mains, rancid frying oil, fermenting garbage, the sweat of millions; second because their guidebook warned, "Breathing Cairo air is equal to smoking thirty cigarettes a day."

Voices in Denise's ear: "Hello, hello. What is your country? Welcome to Egypt, my beauty." Mike's bristling turned most of the men away. There were offers to change money and buy papyrus paper prints, perfume, ancient relics. They left their dreary hotel room and entered a fray, brushing against more people in a day than they touched randomly in a year of living in Davis, picking their way over twisted pavements, around gaping drains, through stagnant puddles.

"Cairo is a personal-injury lawyer's dreamland," Mike said. "A lawsuit waiting to happen on every inch of—they call this sidewalk?"

"Who could pay?" Denise asked. "Anyway, they might not have tort law and damages for pain and suffering."

The Hotel Select was having plumbing problems and water shortages. They were hardly clean enough to have sex; they didn't eat well, or much, and both of them had headaches from the parching heat, the sheets of dust that engulfed them, the slippery drowning in their own sweat. No beer, no wine; only hot tea and occasional lukewarm Cokes. Mike held a warm Coke between his hands and chanted one of Mrs. Cases's favorite sayings: *People in hell want ice water, but that doesn't mean they get it.*

Denise was convinced that good food and cold beer existed in Cairo; it was their failure as travelers that condemned them to greasy, unsatisfying meals and warm drinks. But she had no idea how they might turn themselves into savvy travelers.

Mike didn't complain, and she loved him for this, was proud of herself for having married such a man. Sometimes boring (he liked to retell the plots of science fiction novels in excruciating detail), Mike was solid, generously affectionate, and tolerant. He laughed easily, liked lowbrow movies, and was an excellent cook. Of course, there was his refusal to have children. He thought children were things that might get stepped on, and he hated that they cried, apparently over nothing. Kittens and puppies produced no emotion in him, and he was slightly disgusted by the popularity of baby greens and veal. He knew his view of children was socially unacceptable, and he didn't share it with many. He said his father was like a pesticide continually extinguishing his own fathering instincts. His father *was* extremely unpleasant: mean, biting, stingy. But, Denise thought, that's what therapy was for. Why let a horrible parent ruin your life?

She wasn't waiting for Mike to change his mind. In fact, she'd broken up with him for a short time and put herself back on the relationship market, screening for men who wanted babies. But in bars and restaurants, she began to realize that each of the smiling men sitting beside or across from her was secretly hoping to meet a woman who would take care of him, as if he were the baby. Men were not as cute as real babies, but at least they made an income. In the end, she'd returned to Mike, unable to gauge her own desires. Maybe she wanted children only because she was supposed to want children. She couldn't be certain motherhood was a genuine desire. The powerful pull of what existed—her relationship with Mike—swamped the unknown quantity of child rearing.

They lay together in one of the twin beds, breathing shallowly, Mike holding her loosely from behind, his neglected erection like a tail curled up between her buttocks, their skin wet and strangely cold, as if they were slow-moving reptiles. He beeped and bopped jazz classics into her ear, playing off the street sounds. He was the only man she knew who could enjoy this anti-honeymoon.

Egypt was Denise's idea—her responsibility, her fault. She didn't want one of those sweetly sticky honeymoons, after which connubial life faded like cut flowers; she wanted an adventure, something that would deliver sustainable memories. And, as an adolescent, she'd idolized Nefertiti, the ancient beauty queen with that long, graceful neck and delicate profile, and Cleopatra, who was reputedly not at all beautiful but powerfully charming, ambitious, capable. Except, despite her scheming and intelligence, Cleopatra had killed herself. Denise couldn't figure out what her suicide meant. She had married and remarried and taken lovers and fought wars, but in the end, when Antony committed suicide, so did Cleopatra. When Denise was younger, it had seemed romantic, but now it depressed her. And on the streets of Cairo, who would know if there were women as beautiful as Nefertiti or as capable as Cleopatra? Egyptian women were covered, their faces curtained windows; what did they think of their famous queens, the beautiful and the charming and the powerful? Women whose necks could be seen.

She found herself thinking of their apartment in Davis more and more often, the ease and pattern of their life: Mike's job as a software consultant and hers as an interior design assistant. The air-conditioned darkness of movie theaters; white toilet paper; and a big refrigerator with jars of sour pickles, cold apples, sharp cheddar cheese, crunchy celery and carrots. She was embarrassed by her nostalgia for foods, domestic comfort, the ease of American life. She kept her longing to herself. *People in hell want ice water, but that doesn't mean they get it.*

They went to Luxor by train and checked into another grungy hotel room. Denise decided to wash the gray, flaccid sheets in the sink. She rubbed at the wet cloth and kneaded the pile of soggy sheets like dough, her hands performing motions that seemed programmed into her female genetic code; it was the first time she had washed anything by hand. It was soothing to chafe the fabric in a lulling, repetitive movement, satisfying to twist the sheets into a hard rope, wringing the water out of them. She felt a part of the world, imagining the women of Egypt scrubbing, squeezing, and twisting. Then she hung the sheets to dry on the line Mike strung across the room.

On the ferry across the Nile to the Valley of the Kings and Queens, they passed a stinking, bloated cow carcass floating within sight of people bathing and washing clothes. "You'd think they'd haul that dead thing away, at least for the tourists," Mike said. "Anyway, those people should know better." He was watching some men and boys playfully dunking up and down along the banks, near some reeds, his mouth thin. "The Nile doesn't seem like such a great river. I don't see what the big deal is."

Denise was quiet. He sounded just like her mother, without trying to imitate her.

"It's bloody hot, yeah?" a woman passenger with an Australian accent said. She ran a hand over the soft stubble of her scalp and introduced herself as Amanda from Tasmania.

"I try not to think about it," said Denise. "It makes me hotter, and then I feel I can't stand it another minute."

There was her mother again, in the inflection of her own voice, a shapeless shadow, their Honeymoon Ghost. Did every couple have one—someone agitating the slowly solidifying couple, constantly disturbing the setting Jell-O? "My eyeballs feel sizzled, the air against them like a cooker." Amanda sounded thrilled. Petite and pale, her features were dainty, her body bony, like an adolescent boy's. She was ethereal, tiny, traveling solo; she didn't look like she could survive hot weather or rough travel conditions.

"The temperature is biblical, raising the question: How well can we endure the unendurable?" Mike said.

Trying to wow Angel Amanda. Denise recognized the eager tone, his unmistakable desire to please. He'd taken one humanities class in college and it had been "The Bible as Literature"; now he was going to turn himself into a theologian or historian or something equally preposterous.

Because Mike was staring at her, Amanda explained, "I didn't want to travel with long blond hair, so I shaved my head. Less attention." This was seriously flawed logic, as far as Denise could tell, because Amanda looked so weird that everyone stared. When she and Mike had first seen her on the ferry, Mike had wondered quietly, "A boy on the loose in Egypt? Or, what kind of girl is *that?*" Her head was shaped like a perfect scoop of vanilla ice cream.

They walked white, hot trails behind a guide kicking the hem of his dun-colored gallibiya, the tail of his turban hanging over his shoulder like a braid; how feminine he appeared, in this masculine culture. His name was Mohammed; the Egyptian Everyman. Mohammed explained the Pharaohs' Journey through the Underworld: "Osiris holds the Feather of Truth to your heart—the ancient Egyptians believed the heart was the seat of intelligence—and who's to say it's not? If you were 'true of voice,' you began your resurrection." He looked around at his group of tourists, standing stolidly like overheated pink and white cows. "This, ladies and gentlemen, was the Judgment of Osiris." Denise was more aware of her head, fat with thought, than her heart. What truth did her heart know?

Amanda and Mike launched into a flirtation. Mike was an accomplished flirt; he used his abilities to imitate people, his natural sarcasm to good advantage. Denise felt heavy and lifeless, uninterested in talking to Amanda, a stranger, or Mike, her husband. They entered the dim cool of a mausoleum. Life after death was, at least, cooler than life itself. Everything they looked at had to do with death and resurrection: tombs, mortuary temples, funerary impedimenta, mummification. The excessive concern with the afterlife thrilled and disturbed her. What was the present? A flimsy weekend trip you hardly planned or packed for. Reflection, contemplation, and preparation were reserved for the long trip to the country of the afterlife. Before life, life, after life. Beginning, middle, no end.

Back across the river in Luxor, Denise, Mike, and Amanda drank warm Cokes at a table facing a dusty courtyard with a cracked, dry fountain in the middle. The sun was a knife slammed to the hilt into the day. Amanda lit a cigarette, inhaled, and laid it on the table with the burning end hanging off the edge. She took out her camera and began focusing on the waterless fountain. Denise imagined the picture she would show her friends back in Sydney: a world the color of dust, the sky hot and pale as sand.

A young Japanese couple peered at a menu at the next table, whispering in Japanese. "They can't read the menu," Amanda said, setting aside her camera, inhaling on her cigarette.

They watched silently as the couple tried to order some

food; it was clear that the only language they spoke was Japanese. How many Egyptians spoke Japanese? Denise didn't even know the couple, yet she felt almost sick with sympathy. How did they know anything that was going on around them? They were sightless newborns feeling their way through a scary world; they were moths frantically flapping into bright lights. In all of Egypt, they could count on being understood only by each other—the ultimate couple box. She admired their bravery, their stupidity, their willingness to enclose themselves with each other. But she was breathless with worry. Wasn't everyone in Egypt taking advantage of them?

A horse and carriage careened into the courtyard, the driver, high in the seat, snapping his whip across the scarred, bony back of his horse. They went round and round the fountain, dust rising in billows of cream chiffon, lacing the horse's straining legs and the large spoked wheels of the carriage, then blowing apart. The horse labored, clots of foaming saliva flying from the corners of its mouth. The driver, as underfed as his horse, was intent in his fury.

Amanda went inside the café to get the owners to stop the man. Denise deliberately turned away. The horse and carriage were moving too quickly to make intervention anything but dangerous. Besides, it wasn't their country; who were they to tell Egyptians how to treat their animals? A woman cloaked in black purdah skirted the edge of the courtyard like a skittish Darth Vader. Denise tried to ignore the sound of the whip slapping against the horse's back, the horse's grunts a kind of muffled shriek. She looked into the glass of Coke clutched in her hand, the familiar syrupy color, the bubbles going steadily flat; here was something predictable, understandable—a Coke, losing its fizz. Thank God Coke could be bought anywhere in the world.

Later, in their hotel room, Mike imitated Amanda, flattening his vowels, mashing English until it was almost unrecognizable. *"G'day matey. No worries. That's loovlee."* Denise didn't laugh. She took the sheets, now stiff and rusty from the water she'd washed them in, off the line and made the bed. Then she lay down and closed her eyes. Mike paced the room, perfecting his Australian accent, entertaining himself: *"What're we doing here, Dee? Everybody just wants our money. It's bloody hot. I'm hungry."* He washed his hands, sat beside her where she lay on the bed and stroked her forehead with his wet fingertips. "My wife, my wife," he chanted softly, stroking her with his cool, light touch. She let her eyeballs fall back into her head the way she'd learned in yoga. She collected her brain into the middle of her skull. It was dark and quiet, undisturbed. She didn't know where she was or who she was with.

Her scalp itched. They hadn't gotten showers in Luxor or Hurghada, which meant it had been a week since she'd washed her hair in Cairo.

Boarding the bus to Suez City, Denise counted: eleven days in Egypt, one wretched, tepid shower, two sweaty interludes of sex. They were en route to the beaches of the Sinai. This was meant to be the romantic part of their honeymoon: the white sands of the Red Sea, snorkeling, suntanning, making love. Of course, if great beaches were what they wanted, they could have gone to Hawaii for less money and with better food, air-conditioning, clean sheets—but neither of them mentioned this.

Maybe Suez City would have showers. A famous canal

city, perhaps full of foreigners who required comfortable, dust-free lifestyles. They wouldn't take a room without checking the water taps first. And nothing above the second floor, because she knew by now that water pressure simply didn't exist in the upper floors.

"There aren't any seats." Mike turned as he pushed down the aisle, through people and past a cluster of goats standing shakily, like drunks, over the engine cover. Men's eyes moved directly to her chest or bottom. She sensed Mike react, like a skunk raising its tail. Her figure was far from perfect: curvy but with a little too much flesh. She could take care of herself and she felt resentful of Mike's reaction; he probably wanted to throw one of those black sacks over her head like Egyptian women wore. Marriage certificates and land deeds—no trespassing. But then she softened; in fact, he liked her body, and his response was a kind of respect and admiration. "It's going to be a long ride," he said.

Standing all day. Denise wanted to complain; she wanted to stay in a hotel where she could sit on the toilet seat and trust that the sheets hadn't been sweated in by unknown, unwashed bodies. She wanted to get away from the stares of men. She wanted a hamburger and a salad. She wanted an orgasm or two.

"It's only supposed to be four hours," Denise said.

"Yeah, sure. How these things go, it'll be twice that." Amanda was in front of Mike, her voice cheerful and chirpy. It made Denise sour. Amanda had attached herself to them; they were a threesome, on a honeymoon.

"And we're going to love every minute of it," Mike said. His sarcasm was weary, hopeless.

"What I love is the sense that anything could happen and you don't know what it'll be. It's like Christmas, and maybe you'll get some really horrible gift," Amanda said.

Mike straightened himself and spread his shoulders. Doomed to respond to the human mating dance. Denise knew when Mike didn't like someone, when he was horny, when he was bored. But maybe he wasn't helplessly in thrall to testosterone; maybe he was suppressing a genuine desire to fuck Amanda. What, in the end, could you really know about another person? The dark, hidden interior, full of uncanny mechanisms that kept humans standing on a bus all day. Sometimes she didn't know what she wanted to drink, much less whether or not she cared about having children, or how she felt about Egypt or her husband. When she thought about all the things she didn't know about herself or those she was close to, she felt herself sliding down the slick, red throat of the world into the warm dark below.

But Mike couldn't see inside her either, and this buoyed her. He had no idea that she disdained his adolescent flirtation. That he couldn't resist the coy attention of a pretty woman. On their honeymoon. She sighed. *Newlywed*—such an archaic word, like the '40s or '50s when husbands carried wives with Barbie doll figures over thresholds of suburban houses. Some threshold she and Mike were crossing.

"We're standing, I guess." Denise pushed space in the aisle where she could hold onto a seat back. Mike fit himself beside her while Amanda took a stance on the other side of Mike.

The bus began to move, people still trying to shove their way on board, the driver shouting, passengers straining to see the source of the commotion; a few chickens squawked and then the door squeezed closed, a belt cinched against an overflowing belly. To showers.

But the truth of Egypt was life without water. Once you left the strip of land along the Nile, it was clear that water wasn't just a precious commodity, it was simply absent. Hard, dry land, air furry with dust, thin people and animals. No one awaited the respite of rain. Muffling layers of dust on skin, inside your nose, and on every surface were so ordinary as to be undisturbed and unnoticed. Sentenced to dust.

Amanda was talking. Amanda could talk on and on about everything from Egyptian fashion to Australian television shows, and her talk was charming, but Denise retreated into the tangled mess in her head. This bus full of strangers, the smell of chickens and goats and sweat, of baby pee—it wasn't her life. People said travel expanded your horizons, made you appreciate what you had, but she just felt tired and gassy, petty and irritable. She could get away from all of this, and she felt guilty at the power of her desire to flee.

A baby was crying in the arms of the woman sitting in front of Mike. The woman was swathed completely in black polyester, and Denise wondered if her skin was slimy with sweat beneath all that fabric. The whole affair was shapeless, or impossible to determine its shape; her head was covered, her body and arms, her face, with the exception of her eyes. That small area of skin around her eyes and a narrow strip of forehead were smooth and seductively clear. She didn't have wrinkles, but weariness made her appear aged. And the tiny baby, slack with heat, shrieked in a hopeless wail.

Beside the young woman sat an old man, his mouth half-hidden by a gray beard and mustache. When the old man's eyes drifted toward the window, the young woman flapped at her folds of fabric, trying to get the child's head beneath so it could nurse. But, alert to her movements, the man snapped his head around and slapped her covered cheek. She turned sulkily away, readjusted her material and jiggled the baby in sharp, jerky motions, which only made it cry harder. The baby was hungry; the mother wanted to nurse it; the old man—Denise imagined it was the father of the woman, but perhaps it was an uncle or even a husband, which seemed horrifying since he was old and cruel and she young—wouldn't allow it. Denise examined the woman's wrapping again; it seemed impossible that, in the process of nursing, any part of her body, much less a breast, would be made visible to others. She was so thoroughly encased, it was more likely that the baby would suffocate. Its face was not even wet with tears; flies drank at the corners of its eyes. She couldn't tell if it was a boy or girl.

"*It's not the heat, it's the humidity,*" Mike said in his best Mrs. Case tone. "Not. It's the fucking heat. It's the crying baby. It's the chicken shit on your toes." He looked down at his sandaled feet, where a chicken had laid one spiked foot over a couple of his toes.

Denise shrugged.

The baby wept, the bus rolled on, the heat built.

Then the bus stopped; a sudden silence filled the vacuum left by the cut engine. Denise felt everything that was going on around her acutely. She was aware of how close Amanda was to Mike on his other side; she seemed to have propped herself against him, her hip against his. The bus was crowded, but did Amanda really have to stand so close to Mike? It was too hot, and besides, he was married.

"We're nowhere," Amanda announced in a cheerful voice. She was dipping and ducking to look out the windows. "Yup, big pile of dirt blocking the road. Not even a kiosk selling hot Cokes."

Amanda was talking to Mike, and he smiled down at her, nodding. Denise closed her eyes and drifted. She felt as if her mind would bend, her soul crack, if that baby didn't get what it needed. The sound became part of her;

she felt it move through her veins and vibrate within the nave of her ribcage. The world looked different, as if the crying were a blowtorch, blasting the veneer away. Like Amanda. Amanda looked up at Mike, full of desire, and Denise could see the loneliness that fed her flirtatiousness. It wasn't that she didn't care about his marriage or Denise, it was that she couldn't help herself. And Mike, neither repulsed by her need nor desiring to stanch it—in fact, not having a person in mind at all—just wanted to get laid. Maybe this was why people traveled: for those moments where the world invaded you so thoroughly that it became transparent; she could see into it, like looking into a clear glass of water, seeing all the microscopic creatures and knowing which were deadly.

The bus sat, still and stifling. Hours passed. The door was opened, but few people got off; it was no cooler outside. Instead, they waited without hope or desire for something better. Denise followed their example and found that she stopped being aware of her aching back and the sweat slipping down her chest. Forever seemed real, expansive, strangely benevolent. And the baby cried and cried.

In the midst of a particularly powerful bout of weeping, the woman held the baby up to Denise. Denise looked at Mike for a moment, to register her own surprise, to see what he thought this meant, but he was turned toward Amanda. The woman pushed the baby at Denise's waist, insistent, her eyes pleading, almost belligerent. Denise took the child, cradled it in her arms, and rocked it. The woman never took her eyes off Denise's face, her expression one of fierce concentration, trying to communicate without language. Denise let the sound of the baby's crying bump into her and slide off, like the heat, like her sweat.

"She wants me to take the baby," Denise said, elbowing Mike to get his attention.

Double Happiness

***

THE FOUR PASSENGERS WAITED IN A muddy courtyard while the driver slept off a hangover bought with their down payment. The driver, called Gao Sheng, was Han Chinese and he'd never driven the road to Tashkurgan. He possessed a forged driver's license that said he'd been driving for five years—a lie—and the eight-year-old former People's Liberation Army jeep he was pretending was his own belonged to a friend in the hospital. When he finally appeared, late in the morning, face puffy and eyes red, he'd misplaced the keys.

Gao found the keys where he'd hidden them—and then forgotten that he'd hidden them—in a secret cranny underneath the pullout ashtray in the dashboard. His triumph was muted when he realized that

"What?"

"She wants me to take the baby, give it a better life."

"That's ridiculous. Mothers don't give away their children."

"Sometimes they do. How would you know, anyway?"

"Well, even if she did want you to take it, so what?" His body was tense. "This is so stupid. Why are we stuck on this road? Why not go around?"

Denise continued to rock the baby, loosening the cloth around the tiny neck. "Poor, poor baby. Hot and hungry, and nobody will give you what you want: milk, a cool bath, a quiet dark room."

"I'd want to get rid of that noisy creature," Amanda said.

"Would you, now?" Denise said, staring at Amanda, mentally peeling down into her panting, shrunken heart. Denise allowed disdain and anger into her gaze. One thing she'd learned from her mother: words weren't necessary for communication. Denise gave Amanda a rancorous, unforgiving look. Amanda flushed, glanced off, her face suddenly streaming with sweat, as if she'd burst into tears.

"Can't take care of a baby, can't give away a baby, can't get a shower, can't get a cold drink, can't get through on the road," Mike said.

"Dee," Mike said. He had adopted Amanda's accent; he wasn't imitating her. There was a difference. "Consider the bureaucracy of this kind of thing. Maybe you could be arrested for kidnapping and just imagine what the prisons are like here, considering some of the hotels we've been in."

Amanda laughed.

"Besides, travel with a baby? You can't be serious, luv." He leaned close to her, put his lips to her ear, and kissed her.

She could feel his breath like a feather tickling. His warm breath, which she had inhaled, taken into herself; the inside of his body meeting the inside of her body. His familiar lips, which she had kissed thousands of times. Her unwashed ear, assaulted by baby weeping, caressed by his low, pleasant voice.

She lifted her head. "What makes you think I'm going to keep it? I just know that she *wants* me to take it."

She and the woman stared at each other. They would never be friends, but in a catastrophe, in a war or an earthquake, Denise thought this woman would make a good partner; she seemed more capable of survival than anybody she'd met—more capable of embracing the difficult, the intolerable. She thought of all they shared: body parts obviously, but also the same capacity for desire and disappointment. Of course they were different—they couldn't even speak the same language—and their differences hung between them like a window, but the glass was shattered, milky with splinters. With a stranger, Denise thought, it didn't matter if you couldn't see into them. You never expect to understand a stranger.

The driver started the engine in response to some invisible change of circumstance. Anticipation fluttered through the passengers as the bus moved forward, tilting over the mangled road. Mike said, "We're not going to get to Suez City. We'll have to sleep on the bus tonight, parked in a village that has no running water, no plumbing, no restaurant, no hotel."

"If we're lucky," Amanda said.

"One night," Denise said, "is not forever." Nothing was eternal. Eternal was a concept that meant something, biblically speaking. Eternal damnation. Eternal suffering. Now what did eternal mean?

"I want air-conditioning, a strong shower, a cold beer, a good night's sleep," Mike said.

I want, I want, I want. The propulsion of desire; with-

out desire people would never do anything, neve[r] where or get married or get divorced or have [b] give them away. The woman's fierce stare was [ ]ing. Denise held out the baby—return to sender. married a man who didn't want children; the wh[ ] of taking a child from a woman on a bus in [a] country was absurd; it was too much trouble. Th[ ] a million reasons to hand the baby back. The[ ] sagged, and her eyebrows creased in tiny spasms[ ]tion. And Denise felt the same rush of disappo[ ] She had married a man who didn't want child[ ] either get what you want and feel disappointed[ ] don't get what you want and feel disappoint[ ] sorry," she whispered. A ridiculous phrase, about[ ]ing as the air temperature. There should be a wa[ ] *I cannot help you, because I am not an admir[ ] traordinary person.* Or *I cannot make this ges[ ] raise myself from the swamp of the mundane.*

Denise let her arms hang, feeling the rise and f[ ] inarticulate heart. The world was a feather brush[ ] the dust within, uncovering the hieroglyphics[ ] she could just make out the carved, clear edges,[ ] pressible images. She knew, she understood, w[ ] the windows lay nothing: brown-gray land,[ ] stretches of emptiness, the lonely and the deso[ ] end of human tolerance. The bus's slow mover[ ] ated a caress of air, unbearably hot, achingly so[ ]

one of the front tires was flat. He stood, shakily, staring at it while the inside of his head felt like it was being bludgeoned. Too much beer, too much *baijiu*, too much fun. Had he gambled? He hoped not. He opened the back of the jeep and pulled out the jack. He watched his hands work, fascinated by them; it was as if they had their own mind. He didn't feel in control of his movements, but somehow he was moving. Amazing. He had never changed a tire before, but he acted as if he knew what he was doing. Jack up the car.

The giant, pinkish foreigner stood above him, shouting. Gao ignored him for a while and then, with a snap of annoyance, looked directly into the ghostly face. He didn't trust people with light-colored eyes; they looked scary. Plus, the strange man was pulling so hard at the ugly clump of hair hanging from his chin, maybe it would come off. Gao awaited a ripping sound. The foreigner shouted louder, as if Gao were deaf, when in fact, he didn't understand English. The timbre of the voice was like the wail of a hungry pig. The man was from England, but Gao couldn't remember his name; Western names were not easy. Gao squatted in front of the tire that was suspended in the air and considered it. Hungry Pig paced away, flapping his arms, shouting at his wife, or maybe to her; Gao couldn't tell the difference. Gao looked at her, at her large round breasts, like *baozi*. He wanted to squeeze them, fill his mouth with them; he loved *baozi*. But he couldn't entertain distractions; he had a tire to change. He had to collect the rest of the money, get these people to Tashkurgan.

He found a screwdriver and a pair of pliers in the back of the jeep and stared at the tire again, unsure. Suddenly he felt nervous about this trip. But the money! Four hundred *kuai* was a sum that could make trouble worthwhile. With screwdriver in hand, he popped off the cap at the center of the tire, uncovering a nut with a pin through the middle. He bent back the pin, punched it free, and loosened the nut. He was feeling pleased with himself: things were progressing, it was going to be fine. He was independent, taking risks, making his own money—an entrepreneur.

He'd hung out at the Oasis Café for a few days, offering to drive foreigners as far as Tashkurgan; only officially sanctioned bus drivers could make the journey over the border into Pakistan. As an ordinary Chinese citizen, Gao wasn't allowed to cross any of China's borders. He didn't care that he was leaving his passengers the problem of negotiating the sixty kilometers from Tashkurgan to the border, and then another sixty or so to the first Pakistani town of Sust. Few foreigners were left in Kashgar, most having retreated across China to the more civilized coastal cities. But four people had agreed to pay more money than he would make in three months of construction work, and all he had to do was drive to Tashkurgan. He hoped to find paying passengers for the return to Kashgar. *What everyone likes best is money, but they don't say it,* he thought. He could say it. He even liked *making* money. He would buy a television soon.

He hugged the tire and positioned himself to pull, suffused with confidence. Hungry Pig returned, shouting and waving his hands wildly in an incomprehensible pantomime. Women appeared in windows surrounding the courtyard, laughing at the foreigner—or maybe at Gao, he couldn't be sure. Gao stopped and watched; it was a strange show, he had to admit. Hungry Pig was red-faced and agitated when he finished shouting, and the courtyard was abruptly silent. Gao could smell the Englishman, like something that had been left in an airless room too long.

"What's he saying?" Gao asked the One Who Spoke Mandarin, sitting on a crate against a wall.

"He's insulting China and the Chinese," she said. "And something about how to repair a flat tire. I don't know the words in *putonghua*." She appeared to be thinking. "He seems to think you're not doing it the right way." The One Who Spoke Mandarin laughed easily and had such big eyes that Gao thought she might be an American movie star. He couldn't tell how old she was; not as old as his mother, not as young as the Englishman's wife. The last member of the group was a quiet, serious man who sat on a stool on the opposite side of the courtyard, ignoring the whole tire business. He seemed okay, except he wore his hair like a girl. Only Hungry Pig and Bun-Breasts made Gao uneasy; he was glad he didn't understand them and he was also afraid of what they might be saying.

He resolutely heaved and the tire came off, as well as the central metal drum; a large greasy ball and washer rolled into the mud. He didn't know what he'd done, but he knew it was a mess. Hungry Pig stomped off, putting his head in his hands and muttering to Bun-Breasts. Gao had the terrible thought that if he could understand the pig-like foreigner, he wouldn't have this new, larger problem. *What now?* He stood, wiped his hands on his trousers vigorously, pushing at his panic. *Get help.*

Beth watched the driver walk away from the jeep, still jacked up, parts and tools strewn about; there was a good chance they wouldn't be leaving today. Maybe she'd insulted him by translating Wayne's comment about changing the tire incorrectly, even though she hadn't translated Wayne's ranting on the driver's stupidity. She shifted on the crate; her back hurt. Beth was the only one of the four who spoke Mandarin. The power this gave her was offset by the annoyance of dealing with the Brits, Wayne and Jean, who had, since she'd met them nearly a week before at the Oasis Café, nagged after her to argue with their hotel manager, with the owner of the Oasis, and with the driver.

It was the last day of October, gray skies seeping a feeble, dispiriting rain. She sighed and started a letter to her most recent ex-husband.

Halloween, 1987
Kashgar, Xinjiang Province, P.R.C.
Dear Paul,
   Waiting again. It's been raining for a couple of weeks, and I've been stuck in this cesspool of a town. The concept of drainage hasn't been taken seriously here, and the streets are ponds with thick mud that stains everything it touches. I am being muted into shades of brown. The weather sucks: cold, wet, gray. The kind of gray where you feel you are solely responsible for your failures and unhappiness (the main evidence being the fact that you were fool enough to get stuck in this abysmal town) and your life will never be better than at this single, miserable moment. The kind of weather where you look bad and feel worse.
   An added perk is that there's a hepatitis epidemic and all the restaurants have been shut down. I'm thrilled that the local authorities are so responsible after the fact. So there are peanuts, these baked round breads (called gurdah) that resemble bagels but are drier, and hard-boiled eggs, dyed red to distinguish them from the non-boiled. I probably won't shit for a month, which I suppose is a way of balancing what was happening a few weeks ago. I am thinking of you; if you left the comfort of home, you'd never allow yourself to get mired in such a situation. You'd go for the white-beach-blue-ocean-exotic-fruit kind of travel. I go for the difficult-language-bad-food-nasty-weather kind of travel. I see you sitting on your leather

couch in a temperature-controlled environment
with hot running water and flush toilets nearby,
drinking a cup of coffee laced with amaretto.
Never mind. I'm just suffering a middle-of-no-
where attack. That's where you're so far into
no-place, so high up in the world and away
from your life, that when you look back you
get this vertigo of clarity and regret.
This bit of forsaken earth is as far away from
the world's oceans as you can get. Kashgar is
an oasis town at the edge of the Taklamakan
desert, which means in Turki "you go in and
never come out." Far from anywhere—desperation in the air, unmistakable as skunk
musk. I'm leaving China, even though I don't
have a visa for Pakistan. I think I can wheedle
my way into the country. Pakistan strikes me
as a place where the men haven't seen women
they aren't related to in decades. A series of
big storms—rain here and snow in the mountains—and bus drivers in a snit refusing to
drive, so I'm going by jeep.

It was starting to rain. Beth folded the sheaf of rice paper and stuffed it in her shoulder bag, rose, bent slightly
forward to unlock her stiffened back, and took the split-
board crate she was sitting on into the slim shelter offered by a narrow overhang. Marco, the fourth passenger, watched her from across the courtyard. He was young
and good-looking; she wanted to stare at him for a while
but didn't indulge herself. She also wanted to talk to Paul—
a desire like a headache, like a hot iron pressing the sleeve
of her heart—even though she mistrusted the nostalgia
and regret she felt about him. Perhaps it had more to do
with her current situation than any larger reality. There
was no escape from loneliness.
She sat, staring at the precariously jacked-up jeep, the

sheen of water over mud. The good thing about travel was that there was time to think, to review the past and contemplate the future. The present might be pared down to the vacancy of waiting, or it might be miserable and dull enough that survival demanded a mental detour backward or forward. All that thinking could leave you with a clear mind. The bad thing about travel was that there was time to think. The world faded, and you burrowed into yourself, your failures, your problems. All that thinking could leave you morose and self-critical, isolated. She wanted the truth, the deep, hard, flat, bald, crushing truth. The truth about what? She wasn't sure, but by herself in the world, it felt strangely safe to rip the curtains away from what was hidden in herself. Honesty had a certain appealing adrenaline, like risk, like love. She examined her dirty fingernails, the cracks that petaled the half-moon curve of skin around the top of each nail.

She and Paul shouldn't have split up. They had met at one of her openings at a San Francisco gallery ten years ago. He was stunning, of course: tall, with a handsome dissoluteness that appealed to her. She loved the contrast between his elegantly lanky frame and the practical, thick sturdiness of his hands. He'd never been married, and Beth, who had just divorced her already much-divorced first husband, had been drawn to Paul's insouciant come-hither freshness. He was unpolluted by bitterness, free of wariness. They never did the dance of come-here-go-away, nor did they keep score, secretly weighing and tallying levels of affection—the corrupt banking system of emotional attachment. Now it looked so simple: they had liked each other and spent time together and enjoyed it. She even recalled enjoying their arguments. They married eventually, although Beth was cautious; she didn't see herself as a person with husbands like strands of pearls around her neck. But then, she didn't see herself with the same man forever and ever either. Still, she hadn't wanted to fail with Paul. And when he'd asked her to move out, without acrimony, with the grace and consideration a solid person affords a crazy person, she'd felt like an infectious disease, like the worst thing a man could catch. A year and a half later, she only hoped that the memory of the illness she'd caused in him had faded. She wanted, she wanted . . . what?

The rain stopped; a weak spear of sunshine reached toward her, and she inhaled the stench of mud, listening to Wayne and Jean complaining like a couple of old sows and watching Marco as he leaned, still and beautiful, against the opposite wall.

"Boopers, I have to go to the loo." Jean had one of those voices that scraped against every surface. She and Wayne slumped on a bench under the same overhang as Beth.

"Bloody well go, then." Wayne still appeared sullen after Gao's bungled attempts to repair the flat tire.

"Boo-Purrs. Come with me."

Wayne rolled his eyes. "Why is it that women can't take a pee by themselves?" Wayne spoke loudly, including Beth.

Wayne and Jean were tall, with the plump, spreading hips of comfort and the bitter, wounded, haughty air of deposed colonialists. They had return tickets to London from New Delhi. They could fly to New Delhi from Islamabad, but the only way to Pakistan from northwestern China was by land. Wayne had strawberry-blond hair and a beard of the same color that draped to his solar plexus, which both he and Jean liked to stroke, as if he were a biped poodle. He had a huge chest and he laughed at his own jokes and one-liners, most of which nobody except Jean found funny. She had a mass of black hair falling down her back like a scratchy, woven wall hanging. She was, Beth had to concede, somewhat of a beauty, with perfect English skin, all cream and rose, black hair, black eyes, and a smooth roundness to her features and figure that was appealing if quivery, like pudding. Wayne and Jean alternated between bouts of sticky love and a rancid rage and fearsome dislike of each other. Beth glanced across the courtyard at Marco to see how he was reacting to the Wayne and Jean show, but he had gathered his belongings and was walking away.

She stood, surreptitiously straightening her back so no one would notice the discomfort it caused her, and followed Marco into the street, where donkey- and horse-drawn carts splashed steadily through puddles. He entered a teahouse, and Beth paused to watch the passing scene: women stepped through the mud in thin-soled pumps, and men walked with their heads tucked into the necks of their coats, their eyes on the women. Most places in China, it was hard to imagine exactly how the population had gotten to be a billion. Kashgar was one of the few towns where there was a palpable sexual energy in the air. Here, the faces of the women were tired and giddy, and the men watched them, hungry and brooding. The tension strung between them was unmistakably sexual. She stood for a moment, waiting. There was a kind of waiting that was full of the richness of anticipation, that held the potential for the unexpected as well as the expected. She wasn't just waiting for the jeep to leave. Every moment of waiting contained the possibility of change, large or small, her whole life or merely the course of a day. Something about the randomness of life when she traveled—the way she made decisions that weren't decisions but actions without thought—provided an atmosphere in which she could believe that she might forever after never be the same. She walked through the mud to the teahouse.

Marco was reading a book at a low, wooden table in

the dark, dirt-floored room. What light there was came from the open front, facing the narrow, muddy street.

"Mind?" She ordered a cup of tea and sat down at his table.

He closed his book, gestured to the chair she'd taken. "Please."

She glanced at the book's spine. "Sanskrit," she guessed.

"Yes." He smoothed a hand over the surface, looking at the book with something like love.

"What is it?"

"Buddhist sutras." He smiled at her with a sweetness that made her grip her teacup.

"You're a Buddhist?" Tall and fit, his eyes revealed signs of emotional wear, but his face had the flawless skin of untroubled youth; there were no wrinkles, and he was old enough to have finished with the temporary havoc that adolescence wrought in a face. His straight, thick hair, the color of caramel, was pulled into a short ponytail; his eyes were a combination of brown and gold.

"I'd like to be, but I'm not sure I can be serious enough." He shrugged, as if he were already shaking off his disappointment in himself.

"Why?"

"Why do I want to be a serious Buddhist, or why can't I be one?"

"Both."

He thought. "The answer is the same for both questions: because it's difficult."

"What're you doing in Kashgar?"

"Nosy, aren't you?" he said. "How did you learn to speak Mandarin so well?"

"I studied art in Beijing ten years ago, and I've just spent another six months at the Beijing Art Institute." Her admiration of Chinese porcelain work had brought her to

China long before it was a common place to visit; she'd learned Mandarin because almost no one spoke English. "They say languages are like bicycles; once you learn, you never really forget. How about your Sanskrit?" "I'm a beginner." Again, a dismissive shrug.

At the food stall across the street, a man stood beneath a side of mutton; raw meat brushed the back of his jacket, leaving red streaks of blood across his shoulders. He didn't appear to notice. An old woman walked into the teahouse and stopped to finger Beth's earrings. Behind her came the man christened with sheep's blood, vivid as a photograph. He was wearing a dust-colored shalwar kameez. *Tall, dark, and handsome,* Beth thought in a kind of reflex. With a majestic, substantial nose. It took her a minute to realize that she'd been looking at him too carefully. He stopped, holding his bowl of mutton stew aloft, eyeing her with a mute appetite.

"Listen," Beth said, leaning across the table toward Marco, "I just made the mistake of looking a Muslim man in the eye. He's going to take it as an invitation. Do me a favor and act like you're my boyfriend or husband or something for a few minutes. Okay?"

"Okay." He sounded reluctant.

She leaned back and smiled at him, reassuring, then stretched her hand into the middle of the table. He took her fingers. She laced hers through his. There was the surprise of warm flesh, the dense muscularity of his palm. She realized she hadn't touched anyone for several months; only the random contact of bumping into the billion people of China, more irritating than pleasurable.

The Pakistani found a seat at a table from which he could view Beth. He ate, watching her.

"Where were we?" Beth asked, squeezing Marco's fingers slightly. "Oh, right. You were about to tell me why you're in Kashgar."

Marco looked as if he couldn't speak.

"Darling"—Beth leaned across the table, bringing their clasped hands closer to her chest—"you've held hands with a hundred women. Just flirt with me a little and then we'll get up and leave."

"I came because I heard you could get banana pancakes."

"And the restaurants are closed."

"Right."

"So what's your real reason for being here?"

"What do you mean?"

She was grappling with her desire to stroke the inside of his palm with her thumb. That smooth palm. The perturbed expression that would follow on his beautiful face. She knew her attachment to beauty in men smacked of the shallow, but as an artist, she couldn't help demanding that men be pleasing to look at. Physical beauty elevated the mess of human intimacy; it was about love of beauty, not love of self.

"What I mean is that everyone has a story they deliver about themselves for public consumption. But underlying every surface reason are layers of other, more potent reasons."

"You go first, then." He was beginning to revive and brought his other hand to the table to enclose hers, as if in prayer.

"Fair enough. I'm in Kashgar because I want to see clay forms along the Silk Road. That's the surface reason. I'm really here because I'm not ready to go home and I'm restless; I feel like wandering."

"Why aren't you ready to go home?" Now he was leaning across the table toward her. "Come on, tell the truth."

"It's your turn."

"Is he still watching us?"

Beth ran her eyes around the room, pretending that she

was looking for the boy with the hot water. "Yes." She could feel the heat of the Pakistani man's gaze. A slick of grease had collected in the cleft of his chin.

"I'm here because I'm on my way to India and because I want to see Buddhist art along the way."

"I believe we're still on the surface with that reason."

"I believe we are with yours as well."

Silence fell between them, containing them in an embrace that excluded their surroundings. They loosened their hands, and Beth looked into her teacup, a clump of dark leaves swelling at the bottom of the amber-colored water, her hand curled around the handleless cup, the lacy etching of lines in the skin, the strength and grace of her fingers. The narrow base of the cup rising upward and then turning open at the top like a palm held out or lips parting. Conversation soared around them, the back of the throat sounds of Üighur, the falling and rising shrillness of Mandarin. The boy refilled their cups with steaming water, then sat on a bench nearby, watching them. The present felt dense, impermeable, and for several pleasurable moments, she had that peaceful feeling of being without history.

"Let's go see what's happening," Marco said.

She looked back at the Pakistani as she left the teahouse, though she knew better. And when she saw the smile he had waiting for her, for a moment she hated her weakness, her susceptibility.

Back in the courtyard, Gao was finger painting his pants with grease while talking to his friend. The tire was repaired. "We can go," he said to Beth. Amidst a volley of grumbles from Wayne and Jean about seating arrangements, they got into the jeep, Gao started the engine, and they lurched out of the courtyard. Somebody should have been there to clap, to wave them off, to witness the triumph of departure.

They drove south out of Kashgar; it was midafternoon, and the light wasn't going to last long. The atmosphere in the jeep was tense and excited; it was an accomplishment to get out of town. For Beth, the journey held the unknown and the uncomfortable like a promise of illicit pleasure. Marco sat somewhat stiffly in the back, next to Jean, who sat in the middle. Did he find Jean attractive? Were Buddhists celibate? Years ago she'd shared a house with a couple who rose at four in the morning to sit zazen. They weren't celibate and, apparently, the guy who ran the zendo wasn't either, as he was later accused of having affairs with a large number of the women who pulled themselves from warm beds and walked through the dark to sit facing a wall. The life of the spirit didn't interest Beth; the life of the body mattered to her.

Desire was like swimming in the ocean—once you were in, you were wet and salty and surging with the waves, whether you wanted to or not. She had avoided childbearing and rearing, not wanting to risk losing her looks or take on the accoutrements of motherhood: the carpools and other parents, the utter absorption of interest in one's children. She liked her own interests: art, clay, men, sex, books, movies, traveling, conversation. And giving up those interests for weaning and soccer teams and school districts petrified her with anticipated boredom. She didn't know why her maternal, domestic instincts were undeveloped, but she didn't believe in reforming herself to create them.

They passed a Muslim cemetery, beehive-shaped structures, then red dirt hills. The road was paved for about ten kilometers, and then they slid onto mud. Plane trees loomed, naked and slender as skeletons. Beth sat in the front because she spoke Mandarin, though she felt Wayne's resentment that the best seat had gone to the shortest person. She was glad to be in the front because the jeep lacked shocks. This trip was going to murder her back. She had a herniated disk, which she ignored until the discomfort and pain got to be too much; then she took pills. They were in the flatlands surrounding Kashgar, all the fields fallow with a few soggy remains of the former crop. The mountains stood in the distance, looking plastic and unreachable.

"I'm hungry. I haven't had a good meal since we arrived in China; isn't that right, Boops?" Jean said in a pathetic tone.

"Well, we can look forward to some good curries in India."

"Yes, but that doesn't help right now, does it?" She was looking out at the fields of humped, muddy earth. "I think there's something wrong with these people if they use human waste for fertilizer. Did you know that? Disgusting. Someone has to spread it in the fields; it can't be sanitary work. And then, how could you eat a carrot or a potato, knowing what had been close to it?"

Unlike most Chinese men, Gao didn't smoke cigarettes. Instead, his habit was to hack every five minutes and spit forcefully out the window, rolling the window down and then pulling and rolling it back up with difficulty as it tended to stick and wander off track. Every time the window dropped, cold air hit exposed skin like the flick of a knife. He wore several pairs of pants and a pair of sweatpants layered one over the other, plus a couple of thin shirts and a lightweight jacket. "Will you be warm enough?" Beth asked, partly in earnest, partly teasing.

"I have a coat under the seat." He pointed at her feet, and his eyes followed his hand. The jeep swerved to the right, nearly hitting a donkey cart. Beth yanked the steering wheel to the left, and Gao grabbed the wheel, eyes back on the road, his lips tight in embarrassment.

"Bloody hell!" Jean whined. "He's going to get us killed."

The road was washed out in several places from the recent rains, and they had to make long, circuitous detours through land choppy as a lake in a storm. Oh, her back. They were making slow progress.

"Were you raised in Kashgar?" Beth asked Gao.

He grunted. "No. My family is from a village in Hunan Province."

"How did you get out here?"

He looked at her sideways. "I was in the army. Then I stayed and did different jobs."

He avoided explaining how he had left the army without being assigned another job. In 1987, China didn't offer much in the way of vagabonding. People's lives were strictly controlled, from job to housing to family size. Beth wondered how Gao had managed to drift loose from the iron grip of the Chinese Communist Party. She was impressed by his small measure of freedom.

"How did you get here?" he asked. He wasn't following the standard order of Chinese curiosity: age, marital status, children.

Beth explained about her stints at the Beijing Art Institute.

"And now?" He glanced at her quickly, sharply.

"You mean this trip? Going to Pakistan?" She felt herself flush. "I'm just traveling, taking a vacation." Wander, wander. Destination anywhere. It was profoundly self-indulgent by Chinese standards. She had no purpose, no obligations or responsibilities to anyone besides herself. It was exhilarating to be so unattached, but it left her with the feeling of being shut out of the home of humanity, where everyone was cozy and dull with virtuous self-sacrifice in the name of family. Between Confucius, who had preached filial and social obedience, and Communism, which demanded social loyalty through rhetoric and dogma, she was a freak.

"Do you have brothers and sisters?" she asked.

"Two sisters. My parents are farmers. They all live in the same village."

As the only son, he was traditionally responsible for the care of his parents as they aged. Gao was clearly unusual, having escaped from two dictates of contemporary Chinese life: the Communist Party and filial duty. Beth immediately liked him for it. Plus, he had a certain scruffy charm—spiky black hair, a languid mouth, and keen eyes.

Dusk caught the jeep pitching over a drastically chewed and muddy section of earth, impossible to call a road. They rocked and tilted, nearly capsizing several times. Finally the jeep snapped to a halt, the wheels spinning smoothly in the mud. Everyone got out to look except Jean, who stuck her head from the window and said, "Oh God, Wayne, we're bloody nowhere and it's freezing."

"Fucking wanker can't drive," Wayne said.

The jeep was up to its wheel wells in mud. The sunset cast a solemn, pearled light over the scene. Low, stiff bushes loomed in the dusk, silent creatures awaiting the next event. It smelled of damp, rotting plants and the pungent ferment of mud.

"Maybe if we put branches around the tires, it'll give some traction," Marco suggested. Beth, Marco, and Gao set to work.

"I'll direct," Wayne offered. He snorted in what Beth guessed was meant to be a laugh, but sounded more like an explosion of disgust. He stroked his beard with one hand and waved the other like a conductor, and nobody paid any attention to him.

Gao asked Beth, "What's he doing?"

"Trying to be funny."

Gao looked shocked, then suspicious. "He's your friend?"

"Please don't insult me."

He laughed. "Tell me everything he says. No, maybe I don't want to hear, but tell me some things." He lifted his chin in the direction of Marco's back. "What about him? He's your friend?"

"I've just met him."

"Why does he have girl's hair?"

These kinds of questions were delicate, though they appeared simple. If she said long hair on men was popular in America, he would think all American men had ponytails. But she couldn't wade into an explanation of the '60s, rebellion, anti-conservatism, and the retro-hippie movement that had nothing to do with concepts and everything to do with appearance. Besides, she had no idea why Marco had long hair; it could be vanity. "Some men wear their hair long, each one with a different reason. I could ask him if you want."

Gao considered. "Maybe later."

Jean didn't get out of the jeep because her hands were too cold. "Let's see what the guidebook says." She pulled out a book and began to read in the waning light. "'The area from Kashgar to Tashkurgan dishes up such delicacies as extreme weather and dramatic scenery. It's a two-thousand-year-old corridor for trade, religion, and plunder.'" She paused. "Dramatic scenery? Hard to imagine any good plunder around here, eh?"

"Keep reading," Wayne said, patting his beard.

"Right. 'But the journey to the border with Pakistan is often dominated by breakdowns, crazed drivers, surly officials and frigid temperatures.'"

"Crazed drivers," Wayne said, still working his beard.

"Frigid temperatures," Jean said, looking up at Wayne plaintively.

"Read."

"'The road, seemingly in a state of never-ending construction, suffers from an onslaught of landslides. Expect the full gamut: thick mud, choking dust, and a rough ride that will bounce your kidneys from your heart to your toes. You'll have to work hard to prevent frustration and discomfort from spoiling your experience.' Oh, why didn't we read this before?"

"*We?* You're in charge of guidebooks, Jean," Wayne said. "Keep reading. None of this isn't what we've already discovered."

"'The payoff is the Pamirs, grand and luminous mountains, rising majestically from the plain.'"

"He fancies himself a writer," Wayne said.

"'Upal is the first stop outside Kashgar and your last chance to buy supplies. Keep a close eye on your bags while stocking up on samosas, bread, and melons.'" Jean stopped and looked at Wayne. "Thieves, too."

"Doesn't appear to be somosas within a hundred kilometers. Are we near Upal?" Wayne asked Beth.

The other three were pulling and shoving branches and weeds into the mud around the pits dug by the tires.

"I don't know," she said. She was too preoccupied with the pain in her back, the greater pain to come. But she couldn't stand not being able to do things, as if she were too old.

"I *know* you don't know. I expect you to *ask,*" Wayne said, pulling rhythmically on his beard.

"Do you now?" Beth said. "Prepare yourself for disappointment." What Wayne did with his beard resembled masturbation. She'd call him Jack-Off.

"But, Beth, it's a privilege to hear you speak Chinese. You're obviously quite accomplished, aren't you?"

She cringed.

Gao started the jeep; Marco and Beth pushed. Mud and black exhaust sprayed, but the jeep didn't move. Wayne stood with his hands crossed, nodding his head in satisfied affirmation. Gao said there was a village nearby and he'd walk over to see if anyone could help. Beth volunteered to accompany him, but then they saw lights in the distance pitching toward them.

"What's it going to be, Gao?" Beth asked. She felt obscurely happy, stranded in that muddy field with the sun setting, her hands kneading the pulsing muscle spasms in her lower back. He said something she didn't understand. "What?" Her dictionary was in the jeep.

He said it again, more distinctly, drawing the character in the air. A tractor. It lumbered across the choppy ground, seemingly from nowhere. The world seemed huge, a sea of mud skirting their small figures, the darkening sky overhead, no other sign of life except two disembodied lights bobbing in the distance; the deepening cold of dusk, the warming sense of rescue on the way.

The driver backed up to the front of the jeep and hopped down, the engine throbbing into the surrounding emptiness. He was Üighur and spoke a little Mandarin. Beth understood some Üighur, but there was a relayed translation anyway, from Üighur to Mandarin to English. "We all get in the jeep. He'll take us to his village, over there."

There was some clanking and maneuvering as the vehicles were attached. The two men chatted amiably, as two strangers on a dark, cold night might speak: of the recent rains and the condition of the road. They hacked and spat into the mud. Pulled by the tractor, they slowly bounced across the lumpy field.

A group of people watched the jeep's arrival into their muddy courtyard. After some discussion Gao said, "There is no hotel, only two extra beds in a room. You can share."

"What about you?"

"I sleep in the jeep."

Beth translated. Marco pulled his bag off the top of the jeep and headed toward the designated building. "I'm hungry," Jean said again. "Don't we get to eat? Ask them about food, Beth. Those samosas."

Beth was getting her own pack. They weren't in Upal.

"Come on, Beth, ask about food. You speak Chinese and we don't," Wayne said.

Look, assholes, she privately prefaced her reply. "I'm not your personal translator, and I won't ask for food. This is not a village that even has a hotel, so if they have food, they'll offer it, and if they don't, we shouldn't take it from them. We can go without one meal. Besides, you probably have plenty of snacks." In her pack she had a couple of gurdah hardening into cement, plus some peanuts.

Beth heard Wayne mutter, "Self-righteous Americans."

Beth made a face at Wayne's back, then had to laugh. She was acting like a child, and that was one of Wayne's weapons; he brought out the least appealing qualities in others.

Marco was lighting two candles and trying to get them to stand on the windowsill of the utilitarian room, containing only a pair of single beds and a flowered enamel washbasin. A small room with Wayne and Jean; a single bed she was meant to share with Marco. "There is a certain thrill to sleeping with a stranger in a narrow bed in a filthy, cold room without plumbing or electricity." She told herself she could flirt; flirting was harmless, and it would provide diversionary entertainment as the payoff for dealing with Wayne and Jean. But she couldn't suppress an image of Marco without his clothes on, in the clumsy, sometimes ludicrous maneuverings of sex; all that thrashing and awkward frenzy of flesh. So young, so handsome, so inappropriate.

"Yeah, what would my mother think?"

Exactly. His mother was, no doubt, her contemporary. A woman brought a plate of *baozi*, steamed buns stuffed with scallions and mutton, a thermos of hot water, and two chipped enamel mugs, but no tea.

"Jean, I told you to bring our sleeping bags. Now look at us."

"But we didn't know we would end up someplace without hotels."

"I don't know why I let you do anything. They call this food?" Wayne sneered at a bun. "I hate this country."

"What are you doing here?" Beth asked. Marco pulled his sleeping bag out and left it, still stuffed in its sack, on the bed where Beth had just put hers. He wasn't eating the buns. Weren't Buddhists vegetarians? Love and acceptance for all creatures? A Buddhist wouldn't kill a mosquito if it was about to give him malaria. She looked down at Marco's shoes—leather. How pure a Buddhist was he?

"Why do you want to know?" Wayne slit his eyes.

"You seem unhappy. Why did you come?" It was tedious conversing with someone as contrary as Wayne.

"I'm not unhappy."

"I see." Beth tried not to watch him masturbate his beard: stroke, pull, stroke, pull.

"Her idea," Wayne said.

"His idea," Jean said.

There was a moment of silence. "See," Jean said, turning to Marco sitting beside Beth, "Wayne wanted to buy a motorcycle with a sidecar. He loves bikes, has three of them back home, but none with a sidecar. Isn't that right, luv?" Jean looked to Wayne for confirmation, her tone softened. Wayne petted his beard in silence. "Well, anyway," Jean continued, "the bikes here are quaint, really. They have these lovely pleated little skirts around the seats, usually in velvet."

Wayne put his head in his hands.

Jean went on. "And the sidecars make traveling so easy. Anyhow, once he'd set his heart on traveling by bike, he just couldn't quit when it was impossible, absolutely impossible, to buy that bike. You can't do anything in this country."

"Not true. I gave up the idea and wanted to fly back to Hong Kong and from there to Delhi, but you insisted we keep trying, and now we're heading into the mountains without sleeping bags or any tea."

Beth gave Wayne and Jean some of her tea. "There's probably an extra quilt or two around. I'll find out." She had to escape for a few moments.

Outside, the sky was the kind of black that existed in fairy tales, an impenetrable, troublesome night. The stars were a foggy veil across a cloudless sky. Blessed solitude. It was extremely cold; she felt it in the knuckles of her hands. She squatted slowly against a wall, unkinking her mistreated back, and peed. Then she looked unsuccessfully for Gao. He was probably drinking, which didn't make the morning heartening. It was Halloween in America, she remembered, as she wandered around the village in the dark, looking for someone to ask about bedding, but there was no candy and no trick-or-treating. She found an older, mostly toothless woman who generously loaned a couple of quilts. When Beth returned with them, Marco left.

"What's wrong with him? He hardly speaks," Wayne said.

"He's ducky. Very handsome, don't you think?" Jean giggled.

"All you think about is how some bloke looks."

There was a moment of tense silence between them before Jean said, "Boopers, time to brush our teeth." They began sloshing and spitting. "Time for our pills." They swallowed pills.

"He's got that superior American air."

Jean, with her pristine, unlined skin, her body that had not yet begun to fall or cause her pain, her loud Neanderthal husband. Some men found ditzy women reassuring.

"Time to get in bed, Boopers." They stripped to their long underwear, blew out the candles, and slid beneath the quilts.

"I can't believe I have to go to some Chinese hellhole with a couple of self-righteous Americans loaded with high-tech equipment."

Beth coughed. Wayne was so horrible he was comic.

"Time to kiss, Boopers." There was the sound of their lips, like fish slapping at the surface of a pond. The room was dark.

Beth dry-brushed her teeth, swallowed a double dose of muscle relaxants, stripped, and got into her sleeping bag. She laughed at Wayne and Jean, but their myopic, self-absorbed view of the world was irritating, and only fools would treat someone they needed with disdain. How well would they manage without her translating abilities?

She flipped over; the bed was going to be tight for two people; two people who didn't know each other. She lay still, holding her breath, then exhaling with measured slowness.

She awoke when Marco sat on the edge of the bed. The sounds of him undressing, then his weight as he crawled into his bag. Where had he been? He brought the sharp breath of outside. Her nose was very cold, the rest of her warm. Their bodies were plastered together, shapes blurred by fabric and feathers. It must be the hard curve of his back against her. He assumed a position and then didn't move. His stillness woke her completely; it was uncanny, as if he were dead. She was too old for him; he would never be attracted to her. She could be his mother. A heart-clenching sadness filled her; she felt regret for all she could no longer do, for all she was about to lose. The chaos and anarchy of attraction, the lure of unfamiliar flesh, the entertainment of seduction.

Here lay Beth, forty-five, unattached, with a bad back and a diminishing capacity for attracting men. What if she were to spend her old age alone? She couldn't be sure how this would affect her, whether she would be indifferent, energized by her autonomy and solitude, or simply lonely and depressed. There was a point when she wouldn't be found attractive by anyone, and she was beginning to see this point, as if it were a town she were heading toward. No longer beautiful. Then what? Self-pity was like a gag in her mouth; it made her nauseous and claustrophobic.

She pictured herself lying on a narrow bed beside a man, younger and more beautiful than she was, surrounded by thousands of miles of land stretching in every direction, everything—land, man, bed—unfamiliar. This stark image oddly pleased her, and she slept.

II.

Gao stepped carefully into the courtyard and looked at the jeep, which seemed ready to leave without him, all the bags tied efficiently on top. He hacked and spat, then felt in his pockets for keys, closing his eyes. Bad luck that the sun was out. The guys in the village had treated him like a visiting party chief from Ürümqi, refilling his glass the minute it was empty, asking him a lot of questions. He told stories about the strange habits of foreigners: their smell

(like meat and old eggs), clothes (expensive and tightly
fitted), sexual practices (the women only liked to have the
man behind them or to be on top), and wealth (uniformly
prodigious). Gao didn't know anything about foreigners,
had hardly spoken to one before meeting Beth, but after a
few shots of *baijiu*, he felt like an expert. *Beth.* He said
her name to himself, trying to move his tongue around
the sounds. Maybe she would teach him English, and he
could get more business with foreigners; they had money.

He squinted across the courtyard, trying to evade the
sun and look for *Baozi* Breasts. She wasn't around. What
would it be like to have sex with a Western woman? He
would like a blond, with big breasts, like little mountains.
No blue eyes—they were unnatural. He wanted very pale
skin, so beautiful that white skin, like death; it gave him a
thrill of fright. Long legs, even though he was short. Yes,
definitely, she could be taller than he; he didn't mind. *Baozi*
Breasts had everything except the blond hair. He started
to imagine her long, pale legs wrapped around his hips; his
fingers unbuttoning her blouse, unwrapping those buns.

"Hey, wanker. Are we leaving or are you going to stand
there all morning like the drunk you are?" Wayne came
up to Gao, smiling down at him.

Gao panicked; what did that smile mean? Hungry Pig
couldn't possibly know that he'd been thinking of his wife,
naked. Gao lifted his shoulders and tried to step lightly
and energetically, but he caught his shoe on a stone and
stumbled. The jeep didn't start. He pumped the gas pedal,
turned the key, wanted to mangle the wheel in frustration,
or throw up. It wasn't going to start. His chest clenched
with hatred; the jeep made him look foolish. Then he inhaled, got out, lifted the hood and looked at the engine,
which might as well have been a nuclear power plant.

Wayne stood over him, and the combination of his hangover and Wayne's smell almost made Gao sick. The beard

was talking, shivering and undulating with every incomprehensible word.

"Might be the alternator, but you don't know a goddamn thing." Wayne pointed to parts of the engine.

Gao watched Wayne poke and pull various pieces of the engine and felt the terrible fizzle of inadequacy, as if he were a tire slowly going flat. He knew nothing, and he wasn't good at faking it. He attempted a purposeful, knowing stance. Maybe this trip wasn't a good idea. His head felt like it was cracking into two or three large pieces, like a split melon. The insides were not sweet. Probably he should stop drinking, at least until the trip was over, so he wasn't constantly facing car trouble with the beaten-down feeling a hangover gave him. This was the problem with money: he drank it.

"We need a jump. Go get Tractor Boy from yesterday," Wayne said.

Gao stared at Hungry Pig, frozen in not-understanding. Then Hungry Pig began a strange and careful pantomime. Gao tried to focus on his gestures and movements, but his mind was still drunk, staggering and looping around itself. He wanted to laugh at the big pink man, crouching and flailing his arms, making an animal sound from his throat. Foreigners used their bodies as if they weren't inside of them, nothing like the way a Chinese would use his body. *Concentrate,* he told himself fiercely, and suddenly, elated, he understood. Of course: you needed another vehicle to start a dead one. He went off to find the tractor and driver from the previous night.

Beth found Wayne and Jean sitting on a narrow bench looking furious, desperate, hungry, and nervous at once. Where was the beautiful, the mysterious Marco? She needed the object of her flirtation to be available.

"What's happening?" Beth didn't want to watch the

pendulum movement of Wayne's hand stroking his beard obsessively; this morning it was like a child sucking its thumb.

"Jeep won't start," Wayne said. "I think he's looking for the tractor from yesterday so we can get a jump."

"Maybe we shouldn't even go to Tashkurgan; it might not be worth it." Jean looked ready to cry.

"It's *not* worth it; we're going because it's our only choice," Wayne snapped.

God. Beth wanted Wayne and Jean and their problems with each other to stay in the realm of the vague; she didn't want to view the unpleasantness that underlay their fighting, the petty disagreements and disappointments, the betrayals and secrets. But their marriage was untidy and omnipresent, both unappealing and oddly entertaining.

Wayne tried to wheedle Beth into canvassing for food.

"You're a big boy, feed yourself," Beth said.

"Oh, I'll *feed* myself. I need your charm and good looks to find me the food to put in my mouth," Wayne said, smiling. She suddenly saw behind his faux smile: a lost, anxious boy, worrying about whether or not he'd get to eat. Beth felt as if she'd caught him picking at an ingrown hair around his belly button. He seemed pathetic, sad. What do you do when you see behind a person's mask? She turned her head away, her own feelings too complicated to decipher. "You're not even around when we need you to translate." Wayne stiff-legged across the courtyard and stuck his head beneath the hood of the jeep.

She could easily ask about food; she was ungenerous because she thought he was a jerk. She sighed with self-dislike. Jean was watching Wayne with a detached assessment, as if he were a questionable job candidate.

Marco appeared. "Isn't female modesty a major part of Muslim culture?"

"Yeah," Beth said, "why?" He seemed agitated, speaking loudly and abruptly, furrowing that clear, wide forehead. He was beautiful.

He shook his head. "A man invited me to his house; I had been meditating in what must've been his shed."

"Meditating?" Jean asked.

"And he served me tea with his wife and daughter. At least, I assumed it was his daughter." He looked at Jean absently, and she gave him a flappy, flirtatious smile. He looked away. "He put two large chunks of sugar in this small teacup and then mashed them with a wooden spoon. Like drinking syrup. Horrible. They asked me a lot of questions I didn't understand, but one was probably my age, and I tried to tell them, though I'm sure I mispronounced the numbers. And another was whether or not I was married."

"Standard questions," Beth said. She was distracted by the flurry of smoke that had started in her stomach, rising up through her ribs as if from a fire. She watched his hands, long fingers, a bony thumb.

"They got very excited when I said no, and the mother pulled up her daughter's top, revealing her belly, which almost looked like she might be pregnant, or maybe sick. They talked and talked, and then something went wrong. I don't know what I did or didn't do, but suddenly the father wasn't looking so friendly. I left. Probably more like I fled."

"Ooh. You must've felt just awful," Jean said.

Twinkle, twinkle, sparkle, sparkle. Beth didn't want to witness Jean's attempts to flirt with Marco.

He looked at Beth. "They *showed* me her bare belly; I didn't *ask* to see it."

"You think they wanted you to marry her? Cure her?" Beth asked. Why was he upset? It seemed like an odd experience, but nothing bad had happened. Maybe she'd

missed the point. She inhaled an admonition to herself:
Pay attention, no boys, just travel.

"Why would they ask such things of a total stranger?"

"I almost never expect to understand someone from
another culture. When understanding occurs, it's like
grace. When it doesn't . . ." The impossibility of human
understanding. A yawn of loneliness lifted her insides. She
hadn't understood Paul, someone who spoke her own language, who grew up in her country. Life was planted in
the mysterious. Part of the reassurance of being a foreigner in China was that she was obviously an outsider,
misunderstanding was assumed. She couldn't even be critical of her own failures. She expected to make mistakes in
another country, in a foreign language.

The sun raised a head of steam off the mud. The air
took on the warm, heavy scent of wet earth. Marco, looking dazed and uneasy, wandered off; Beth sat beside Jean,
who took a compact out of her bag and looked at herself,
moving pieces of hair around. "I used to be pretty," she
sighed. "Now I've got dark circles under my eyes, and my
skin color is off, face puffy, hair dirty. I'm a wreck." She
glanced over at Beth. "Thirty minutes in a clean bathroom and I could do myself back to normal." She sighed
again. "Not that anyone would care." She clicked the
compact closed and stuffed it back into her bag. "Especially not my charming husband." Her glance flicked to
Wayne's back, her voice with a distinctly snide tone. "Are
you married?" She turned to Beth, sprightly now that she
was off the topic of herself.

"No."

"Not ever?"

"Not recently."

"You don't have children, do you?"

Beth looked at her, trying to gauge the motive behind

this question, but then decided she was being paranoid. "No." She didn't want to talk to Jean, to get to know her or find her sympathetic. She sensed a desperation in Jean that made Beth uneasy, afraid she might recognize some part of herself. She didn't want to have anything in common with Jean except certain obvious physical configurations.

The tractor rolled into the courtyard. "Oh goodie, car repair," Jean said.

The three men hooked the jeep to the tractor's engine. While it was charging, Wayne started the jeep, eyeing the dashboard. "It's not charging!" he shouted, shaking his head violently. "It's definitely the alternator." The engine began to squeal as if it were a small creature being tortured. Wayne gestured for the tractor driver to give him the dagger tucked into his belt. The driver suspiciously relinquished it, and Wayne used the tip to draw in the mud the tool he wanted. The driver pulled his tools out, and Wayne chose the one that most resembled his drawing. Beth felt he was intentionally snubbing her ability to translate. *Fine.*

Gao watched, impressed, as Wayne expertly tightened and loosened and pulled at things with complete confidence. They jumped the jeep again, and this time the battery showed a charge. Wayne nodded his head, satisfied.

They left the village in the early afternoon and drove through a stark, gray floodplain bent by the slow washing of the Ghez River, sheer rock walls ascending on either side. It was a spine-shattering drive, and as they climbed higher, the road was dry, creamy dust clouding their wake. Wayne insisted on the front seat, so Beth, Jean, and Marco shared the back. Beth shifted constantly, trying to help her back to relax, but the violence of the vibrations prohibited any respite. She was taking painkillers as well as muscle relaxants.

Gao stopped every hour or so to apply cellophane tape to the cracks growing in the windshield; he drove badly, shifting in jerks and braking in frantic stabs. He was severely hungover, pale and shivery. The inside of the jeep was a stagnant pond breeding a crop of unidentified bad feelings, making the landscape out the window seem unreal, out of reach. Beth clamped her headphones over her ears and let herself disappear into Colombian salsa. Camels grazed in the distance, and a singular clump of trees stood, elegant and thin. Groups of scruffy road workers sieved rock by hand through screens. Wearing torn, navy blue Mao jackets over bright pink T-shirts, they looked cold and wind chapped. Their camps were bleak groups of beige tents flapping in the wind like trapped birds.

"Convicts," Beth said, louder than necessary because she was still wearing headphones. Gao jolted to a halt, the road was blocked. Beth removed her headphones.

"They're dynamiting ahead; the road is still under construction," Beth translated. There was a moment of strained silence, and then Wayne started a fight with Jean. He blamed her for their awful trip; she tried to calm him, calling him Boopers in a pleading tone. They seemed to have forgotten that Marco and Beth understood everything, or maybe they didn't care, or maybe they liked an audience. Apparently this was their *vacation* ("Northwestern China a vacation?" Marco whispered), though Wayne had wanted to go to Thailand because Thai women were so attentive. Then it was Jean's turn to be furious. Beth and Marco looked at each other, then got out of the jeep— Beth trying to move as if her back weren't a clenched fist— and Beth asked Gao to pick them up farther on. He gave her a nervous, frightened look. She told him to ignore

Wayne and Jean; they were only quarreling. At least he didn't understand their nonsense. When Beth slammed the door, the shouting inside didn't even pause.

"Those two are a bad advertisement for the joys of traveling as a couple," Beth said.

"They're struggling," Marco said. The road they walked was composed of small rocks sieved by hand.

"Struggling? They're irritating, obnoxious, unpleasant."

"Yes. But in the end, they are just human beings, unhappy and unconscious."

"Are you one of those people who are always nice and forgiving?" Beth asked. God help her—a handsome, sanctimonious boy. She took a deep breath, cold air cutting through her nose, her lungs tight, the air noticeably thin.

"No, but I try to practice the art of compassion."

"Mmmm." She felt cynicism ready to break out like a rash. Good people bored her. She glanced at him suspiciously, wishing she could crack him like a piñata and see what fell. It wouldn't be all candy. Spiritually pristine people always harbored some festering ugliness.

The road workers stared, particularly at Beth; they didn't realize she understood them. "Tell me what they're saying," Marco said.

"Okay, but it's not going to be compassionate," she said. "'Two foreigners coming this way,'" she began.

"'One is a woman.'

"'I want to fuck her.'

"'Me too. I've never done it with a foreigner.'

"'He's nothing to worry about.'

"'He looks like a girl.'"

"Because of my hair?" Marco interrupted.

"I imagine," Beth said.

"Are they dangerous, or just boasting?" Marco looked back toward the jeep, which wasn't in sight.

"I'm sure they're dangerous, but we're foreigners; it's all talk." In the past, this corridor through Central Asia had been rife with thieves and murderers, a fraught passageway through the mountains, over distant borders. A spasm of apprehension gripped her. People didn't change much; did places?

Then a short, wiry man broke away from the group and waved a stick of dynamite at Marco and Beth. Marco instinctively dropped into a crouch. "It's okay," Beth said and translated the man's hoarse cry: "'We'll show them how great China is; even prisoners can blow up mountains.'" Then the man laughed until he started coughing. Marco and Beth stopped while one man stuffed dynamite into prepared niches and packed gravel on top of the charge. Several others laid the wires from the charges out flat where they connected at the fuse. When it was all prepared, they frantically motioned their audience to move back and get down. Marco and Beth kneeled behind some boulders. A deafening series of explosions and the hill spewed gray rock, airy as foam. Dust fell. The mountainside, which had protruded into the road like the tongue of a glacier, was completely gone. Beth had never seen landscape changed so utterly, so quickly.

They picked their way through the rubble and continued up the road. A hard, clear light cut across the land, illuminating three camels against a field of snow. The sound of their boots against the rocks was like ice cracking.

"Were you raised a Buddhist?" she asked.

He shook his head. "My parents are old hippies. Before I was born, their religion was psychedelics. After they had kids, they couldn't bring themselves to do the church thing, so they decided they were atheists. I learned to meditate from a Buddhist priest who sang in a thrash rock band. He was amazing. He was very nearsighted, but once I

saw him pull two finches, loose in a room, out of the air.
He caught them without effort. The world was transparent to him; he could see behind things."

"What happened?"

"He died."

"Was he old?"

"No. In his thirties. The doctor said he died of something that came in with the wind."

"Well, there's one real reason behind your presence in this far corner of the world."

"Yes."

"But there's more, isn't there?" She felt sure he was escaping something, and it wasn't the death of his meditation master.

"Your turn."

"I want to travel light and cheap before I can't do it anymore." Enjoy freedom and detachment before the enjoyment faded, before her back, even with pills, couldn't tolerate a journey like this one.

He looked at her sharply. "Because of time and work obligations?"

And age and the death of desire and social pressure and the crushing inertia of loneliness. "Yeah. Are Buddhist monks celibate?" she asked.

"Depends on the lineage. Each lineage has different vows, precepts, and prohibitions. Like in Teravadan Buddhism, monks eat two meals a day, and they must beg and not consort with hermaphrodites."

"Hermaphrodites? Shouldn't be too hard to avoid. You're wavering; perhaps you'll be celibate and perhaps not."

"Not exactly. I've chosen celibacy."

"Are you going to shave off your beautiful hair?"

"Yes. Head shaving is the cutting of attachment."

"What is it about an ascetic life?"

He smiled.

Gao yanked the jeep to a standstill, spraying them with pebbles. Jean had her nose practically glued to the window, the back of her hair messed into a big knot, as if it had been chewed. Gao was chattering to a taut, compressed Wayne. "You are the Big Man. Yes, I want to be like you, a big man who can defeat his little wife." Gao's laugh seemed to scrape its way out of his throat.

Beth asked what had happened.

"I don't know; I don't speak English."

"Did he hit her?"

"No, he made her weep. Like a good husband." Gao laughed again. "He can fix an engine and make his wife cry."

The climb into the mountains was slow, the jeep's engine grinding and lurching. The Ghez River canyon narrowed, pinching the river into a steep, wild spill over boulders flecked with froth. The peaks on either side tweezed the sky into a tidy strip of lead. At the checkpoint, a guard examined everyone's papers, flipping the pages and turning to peer at various visas for his own entertainment. A single adobe hut stood at the edge of a drop to the river. Wayne and Jean took photos of each other standing in front of the pole slung across the road. They didn't ask anyone to take a photo of them together, but Beth saw Wayne try to smooth Jean's hair before she stood for the photo. He patted the tangled mass on her head with an awkward tenderness; he seemed regretful, embarrassed. Gao talked to the guards, laughing too loudly. Marco walked around the corner and stood above the river.

Strangers in a jeep. Beth felt tired and heavy: something was wrong. If she were reporting this trip to Paul, she would make it humorous, turn the tension with the fork of wit. But Paul didn't care about her troubles or require her entertainment; he probably loved someone else by now. After a year of murky phone calls and half-movements toward and away from each other, he'd asked her not to call or write because he needed a blank space in order to forget about her. She'd sent him a postcard telling him she was going to China and giving him an address in Beijing, in case he wanted to write her. She hadn't heard from him. She wrote him—she couldn't help herself—but she never mailed the letters, just let them collect in her pack, held together with a rubber band. It was a monologue without an audience, like hoping to communicate with the dead.

The landscape grew harsher and more desolate. Snow-frosted sand dunes loomed at the edge of a snowy field. Beth's toes became numb; her back was in agony. They passed a few stone huts without any smoke coming from the chimneys. There were yaks, Bactrian camels, two ponies. The sun set, mountains fired a soft pink, then a murderous, seeping blood color, then the cold blue of dusk and finally, black night. Gao drove without headlights, peering into the moonlit night hunched over the steering wheel. Wayne went rigid at this new and unusual driving method. Jean's face was ghostly, one cheek yellowed in a slash of pale light. Sight of Jean's sad, deflated expression triggered Beth's own curtained-off despair. She couldn't tolerate signs of heartache and disappointed love in others.

"Bulunkul." Gao pulled into a compound with a red star over the gate.

"I hope there's something decent to eat," Wayne said.

Inside the main room, two ill-tempered men greeted them. They made Gao move the jeep to the opposite side of the courtyard for no reason, charged four *yuan* for each person to spend the night, and the larger one, dirty apron circling a thick waist, escorted them across the courtyard with a kerosene lantern. There were doors all around the courtyard, though no one else appeared to be staying there.

He ushered them into a cavernous room, large enough to sleep forty. Cold wind rattled loose panes in the windows. Unwashed quilts were stacked in one corner; the floor was dusty concrete. There were no beds. After the man left with the lamp, the room fell into gloom and moon shadows. Wayne began settling in the corner with the quilts. Jean didn't move, her face stiff and gray. Beth told them there was a little food and some boiled water for tea. Wayne said, "Hurry, Boops, let's get something to eat before it's gone." As if there were a crowd. Because Wayne and Jean were a couple, Beth and Marco became a pair. They set their pads and sleeping bags down beside each other in the farthest corner from Wayne and Jean.

Beth and Marco drank tea and ate plain, tasteless steamed buns in the dining room. There was a poster of a soldier on horseback—whom Beth recognized as Zhu De, a Red Army hero—amidst a grove of pink plum blossoms on one blackened wall. A kerosene lantern sent oily smoke to the ceiling. The table was sticky.

The room was filled with the sound of chopsticks scraping against bowls. Wayne and Jean ate silently, shoveling in gray rice and greasy cabbage. When they finished, Wayne took Jean's hand. "Let's go to bed."

"I want to write a few postcards," Jean said, pulling her hand back.

His moment of sweetness disappeared, and he looked as if he wanted to slap her. The bench screeched as he pushed away from the table and left. Marco closed his eyes and began to inhale and exhale with a determined rhythm. Beth went to lean against the doorjamb to the kitchen and talk to the cook.

Jean arched her neck and looked across at Marco. "What're you doing?"

"Meditating."

"Oh." She giggled, then pitched her voice higher. "Do you have a girlfriend?"

"No." Marco opened his eyes.

"What's a handsome bloke like you doing without a girlfriend?"

"Traveling."

"That's wasteful."

Beth wanted to see Jean's face, but she couldn't.

"I wish I smoked; I need something to do, something different," Jean said.

Marco nodded, then grabbed his bag and fled.

Gao came into the kitchen, and the cook slopped rice, cabbage, and a bit of pork into a bowl. "Did you eat?" Gao asked Beth. The Chinese had a preoccupation with food that rivaled that of the Italians.

"Enough. Where're you sleeping?"

He shrugged. "It doesn't matter. The jeep is fine, too, you know." He lifted his chin. "I'm going to sit down."

The cold outside hit Beth with a refreshing slap. She walked to the outhouse up the hill behind the courtyard. The moon hung, a fat and incongruous ornament in a stark and empty world. Night was around her, big and cold and lonely; she felt as if there were nothing between her and the world, no buffer. She might die of exposure, or of loneliness. Whenever she'd been without a relationship, she'd relished the feeling of being in the world by herself; an elegantly solitary unit. But lately she couldn't tell if her presence mattered without anyone to show her— she was an appendix in the belly of the world—and she was left with a shrunken feeling, the soft creep of desolation. She did some slow, painful stretches to loosen her lower back, looking at the dark sky and the dark earth.

The outhouse was made of flaking bricks, without doors of any kind. In the beam of her flashlight, she found a dead bird lying in the entryway. The facilities were two holes cut into the concrete floor. One of the incomprehensible aspects of outhouses in China struck her anew; piles of turds littered the floor like arranged sculpture, or some oblique message. What they were telling her: *step carefully.*

Gao entered the dining room and *Baozi* Breasts patted the bench beside her. She was smiling at him. He felt too nervous to sit beside her, so he sat opposite. She stared at him as if he shouldn't have sat down, and he felt the twisting of doubt in his belly. Foreigners were impossible to understand. She pulled a small book from her bag, selected a page, and handed it to Gao. It was in Mandarin and English. The section was called "Making Friends." Gao read one of the sentences aloud in Mandarin: "Do you mind if I sit here?" She giggled and tried to repeat what he'd said, but it sounded nothing like Mandarin. Not a single word was actually a word; she just made noises, like a bird. It made him laugh, so then she read in English: "Why are you laughing at me?" And when he tried to pronounce the words, she laughed. They went through several sentences, reading the translations and laughing because neither of them could pronounce the other's language. She was so beautiful it made his body cramp and ache. He was uneasy about some of the sentences they practiced. Why did she choose "Would you like to go out with me tonight?" Or "Where shall we meet?" They read only questions, no answers. He wanted a drink, but he couldn't leave, pinned down by those enormous breasts. He couldn't stop imagining how they would look unwrapped, how they would feel in his hands. He felt sick, like a hangover, drunk with uncertainty and fear. He'd never had a Chinese girlfriend, and sometimes he worried that he wouldn't know what to do when the time came. He'd slept with a whore twice when he was in the army—it was dangerous and not entirely pleasant, though not terrible either. He was grateful for even that minimal, unsatisfying, slightly frightening experience. It was better than never having done it at all. Now he was flirting with a married Western woman. He almost groaned aloud. Maybe the big husband would attack him in the night; the risk he was taking made Gao giddy. He could smell his sweat, strong, like a water buffalo. So much of his life had been dull, plodding, uneventful; never again.

Beth awoke in the night, her back hurting. It was cold, the room soft and foggy. There had been a noise, maybe a gunshot, and it had startled her, set her heart beating. She'd been dreaming of making love to Marco, pulling his shirt over his head . . . She closed her eyes, let her mind deliver its imaginary scene, let her body sink into sensation. Music blew into the room in uneven gusts—a low bass rhythm and a high-pitched melody. Marco was beside her; she could touch each of the parts of him she was seeing in her mind, and he could touch her back. Eyes still closed, she turned toward him, lingering over the details, breathing in his smell. She stopped herself, held her breath. Not Marco. It was an accident of attraction. She felt herself drifting down a sinkhole of dismay and self-reproach. This was the place she was traveling through, where the ground was thin and the air pale, and things seemed too opaque to be tangible, an indeterminate landscape where direction and destination were meaningless. She would get older but no wiser.

Marco rolled over, with a sound between a gasp and groan. She could see his face in the moonlight, the earnest crease of his brow confused between pleasure and pain.

He mumbled, incomprehensibly, except for one word: "Emily."

III.

At dawn Gao stood in the courtyard watching snowcapped Mount Kongur turn flaming pink. Cold air clung like ice in his lungs and throat. Raw silence surrounded the empty courtyard. The village of Bulunkul—a few mud buildings—perched on the hillside parallel to the courtyard. Without the filter of a hangover, the landscape seemed too beautiful. It made his heart sad and small. He was up before his passengers and he looked around, fiddling with the keys in his pocket, ready to drive away. He couldn't keep a nervous smile off his face. He was in trouble; he felt happy, as if he could strip naked in a snowstorm and withstand the shock. The mountains waited as the sun rose, igniting their snowfields into a pure, white-blue light. He bounced on his toes a little, to feel his cold feet, then got his tea jar out of the jeep and went to the kitchen to fill it with hot water.

No sign of Wayne or Jean, no sign of Marco, no sign of Gao. Beth put her pack on top of the jeep, walked to the courtyard entrance, and stood, shivering. She thought of walking down to the irrigation ditch in the dried meadow across from the courtyard. She thought of going up to the outhouse. She felt tired, indecisive, grimy, disturbed. The pain in her back was her ghost companion, called misery. She ignored it, and then pain asserted itself, and she remembered, *Oh yes, I've brought my bad back on this trip,* and she tried to stuff it into the bottom of her pack so no one would find out. Plus, travel in China wasn't conducive to an affair. She wasn't clean, didn't feel appealing or alluring; she certainly wasn't flirting with conviction. Marco was beautiful, dull, too young, and still her mind drifted into schemes of sex, scenarios of seduction. She wanted to put a hand against her own nose, *Down, Beth, down,* as if she were an ill-trained puppy, jumping on strangers, getting close to the wrong people, with no sense of boundaries or how to behave in mixed company. Who was Emily, anyway?

Her marriage to Paul had been fine, not as in "just fine," but as in the fineness of linen, or silk. And its demise was clearly her fault: Paul's defection triggered, finally, by a Trinidadian named Clive whom she'd picked up at a hot springs. Clive hadn't been the only one; he was simply the one at which Paul had calmly said, "You are a person who shouldn't be married." And then he'd stopped being married to her. She admired long-term relationships; she was impressed and amazed by the concept of "forever and ever." But she didn't understand what it took to endure life with someone when it grew familiar, unexciting and routine. Why couldn't she be faithful to someone she loved? She was a bad person who, deeply embedded in middle age—the age of reason, maturity, and bad backs—had not yet learned to relinquish the irresistible irresponsibility of youth. She was miserable about the mess she'd made of her marriage with Paul, but her misery hadn't affected her relationships with men. Desire, like some kind of mutant emotion, continued to thrill and haunt her. She was sick of herself, and this was a hard thing if you were traveling alone.

Then, abruptly, standing in the cold, the last thing she wanted was a beautiful boy to seduce. She wanted a hot shower, a plate of warm toast and fresh fruit, and a scalding, sweet cup of coffee. Perhaps here was the impetus to shift into maturity, a pursuit of comfort over desire.

Gao sauntered from the kitchen, letting his hips rock back and forth. He set his jar of tea on the hood of the jeep. Stretching luxuriously, he rubbed his belly, smiled, and called out, "It's cold, isn't it? And so beautiful. My mother would never believe me if I told her I was here, in a place with no trees." He swept his arm in a wide circle, indicating the open stretches of land and huge peaks. He hacked and spat with satisfaction. Jean marched out of the big room, threw her pack on top of the jeep, and, head down, strode through the gates. Gao watched her like she was a deer in his sights.

"What's wrong with her?" Gao asked, and his laugh sounded like a shriek. After searching through the jeep, he pulled out a smashed packet of cigarettes, shook one free, and shoved it between his lips.

"I thought you didn't smoke," Beth said.

"Today, I begin. Do you have a match?" The hand he held out trembled.

She pulled a box of Double Happiness matches from her bag.

He began rummaging in the jeep again. "Maybe you should follow her. She could get in trouble!" he shouted, his head beneath the front seat.

"What do I care?" Beth said in English. She didn't want to take care of anyone else; that's why she'd avoided motherhood. Gao raised his eyebrows. She translated: "What kind of trouble is out here? Maybe she'll fall into the irrigation ditch and get cold feet."

Gao was trying to inhale smoothly, but he had to remove the cigarette and cough. He avoided Beth's eyes, and she knew that something had happened.

Within an hour everyone was in the jeep. Gao was spitefully blowing cigarette smoke at the dashboard and coughing convulsively in the direction of Wayne's lap. Wayne and Jean stared ahead, their faces carefully expressionless. Marco was unruffled. He probably meditated before dawn, returning with this look of unshakable peace. How exasperating. She wanted to seduce him if only to disrupt his unperturbed façade, to challenge his complacent celibacy, which seemed unnatural in a boy so handsome and young.

The day clouded over, turning the shadowed snow ashen. The jeep started raggedly, spewing black smoke. No one mentioned food; no one was around to provide any. Gao drove through the gates and turned south, back onto the rocky, pitted road. This was the last sixty kilometers to Tashkurgan. The town sat in a knot of borders with Pakistan, Afghanistan, Tajikistan, and Kyrgyzstan, meeting in a tangle of high, desolate peaks. The forgotten far edges of countries; areas that few visited and nobody cared about.

A dead dog lay twenty yards down the road. Gao grunted, fumbling with his cigarette and the gear shift, nearly singeing the back of Wayne's hand in his clumsiness. He seemed undecided about whether to drive around the animal or over it, and he certainly didn't know what to do with his cigarette. Wayne yanked his hand away and looked like he was going to hit Gao. Gao clamped the cigarette between his teeth, downshifted, and gunned the engine. They lurched over the dog. The tires met resistance, and then there was the soft give of flesh. It was too cold for flies. Ash fell in his lap.

"Was the dog shot?" Beth asked Gao. She remembered the wind picking up in the night, playing at loose edges of the building in unsyncopated percussion. And then a sound that might've been a gunshot. The room had been cold, catching the full force of wind. The thin sounds of music blew in; a throbbing, low-toned music. And Marco talking in his sleep.

Gao nodded, but how would he know?

"Why?"

He said a word she didn't understand.

"Say again." She pulled out her dictionary, while Gao repeated and fingered the shape of the character in the air with his cigarette, the jeep wobbling. What a disaster that he'd decided to start smoking; Gao was a bad driver without a burning object in one hand. After a few moments, she found it: *rabid*. Still, that hardly explained shooting the dog in the middle of the night. She showed the page to Marco and took a moment to look at him carefully; that smooth expression encasing some inarticulate mess.

They climbed through a long valley, giant boulders strewn like sculpture in sloped pastures. The river was serpentine, a sea green. They wound up and leveled at Karakul Lake, coin-flat and silver at the base of Mount Muztagata. Smoke rose from a cluster of mud buildings. The plateau beyond Karakul was dotted with yaks and camels. The beauty out the windows was a harsh contrast to the clot of festering tensions within. Beth felt a headache building. Wayne and Jean were getting uglier. Beth had no affection for them, but she felt a moment of empathy, recalling a few miserable road trips she'd taken with her first husband, where the inside of the car resembled a petri dish sprouting a deadly virus.

Around a curve in the valley lay Tashkurgan, a bleak, dreary spit of human life.

Bulunkul to Tashkurgan was the shortest leg of the trip, so it was noon when Gao pulled into the courtyard of the Pamir Hotel. He cut the engine, and the flat silence in the jeep made Beth shiver. "Now what?" she asked Gao.

"Stay here tonight, you find a ride to the border, I leave in the morning. That is best," he said.

"Okay. I'll find out about rooms," Beth said, and Marco

followed her. When they were clear of the jeep, she said, "Someone's going to blow. You think Wayne's capable of violence?"

Marco shrugged.

"Think he'll go for Gao or Jean?"

"Gao."

"What should we do?"

Marco flipped through a thin paperback he'd been reading in the jeep, opened to a page, and read, "'To preserve your life you must destroy it; having completely destroyed it, you dwell at ease. When you attain the inmost meaning of this, an iron boat floats upon water.'"

"So?"

"There's nothing we can do."

"You know, this just might be a time for action."

"Doing nothing is doing something," Marco said.

Closer to Buddhism than she ever wanted to be.

At the front desk, a Tajik woman with long braids and an embroidered red vest scowled. Her face was plastered with thick, powdery makeup, thin lips and eyebrows slashing through the field of white. She practically yelled at Beth.

"She insists she has no rooms, but she's lying. Of course there are rooms; there is no one in this town," Beth said. Nobody came to Tashkurgan for itself, and no buses were making the trip over the border, which was about to close for the winter anyway. Hotel clerks in China routinely lied about such things—to take pleasure in their small measure of control and power over others, or for some other reason; Beth didn't know.

Marco was staring at her fixedly, as if she were the object of his meditation practice. She had an urge to punch him, pictured her fist in his solar plexus, landing in that hollow men had where the two sides of their rib cages met. She wished he weren't so serious. It would be good if he could tease her; she was pleased at the possibility of humor surging beneath his plastic coating of Buddhism.

Beth negotiated further. "She admits she has rooms, but only at a hundred and seventy kuai a night." This was an outrageous sum of money.

"Is there another place to stay?" Marco asked.

"No." Beth felt just as combative as the receptionist, which was a mistake. "We'll return later." She knew from experience that it wasn't possible to win battles with officials or clerks in China. Even when she got what she wanted, the emotional price always proved too high.

In the courtyard, Wayne was languishing against the jeep's hood, a sly smile on his face. Gao sat smoking on a bench against a wall, and Jean was nowhere to be seen.

"What about the rooms?" Gao asked, staring hard at his cigarette, in a pose that made him look as if he'd been smoking for a decade.

"One hundred and seventy kuai."

"They are bad eggs here," Gao swore and spat thickly.

"Where's Jean?"

"Why would I know?" Gao snapped, then looked embarrassed. "She went to the market."

"Gao." Beth inhaled deeply. "Did you have sex with Jean?" She hoped he'd be honest—lying was a national survival tactic in China; everyone agreed it was both wrong and necessary—though she wasn't sure she wanted to cope with the truth. He nodded.

Shit. Beth sat beside him, wondering what he'd thought of his first sexual experience with a foreigner. "Does Wayne know?"

"Maybe," Gao said. "He doesn't like her."

"Don't be silly. He wouldn't want anyone else to like her."

"She's sad and nice, but I don't care about her." He

cared about making money, about buying a TV, about getting back to Kashgar. For some reason he felt like crying, and this embarrassed him, so he focused on the cigarette. What a wonderful invention cigarettes were.

"Gao, I don't have a good feeling about this."

He shrugged, as if he were already sentenced.

The Tajik woman approached Beth, offering to show her a cheaper place.

The woman, Beth, and Marco walked abreast down the unpaved streets, turning heads as they passed. Strangers got a lot of attention in this small town. They arrived in an abandoned courtyard and turned down a dank hallway with rat droppings in the corners. The Tajik woman showed them two rooms, each with broken window glass on the floors, two filthy mattresses, cigarette butts, and assorted debris. "We're going to be squatters. They're not worth ten kuai," Beth said flatly. She argued heatedly with the woman. "She'll go down to seven."

Beth paid, and the woman gave her keys, which seemed utterly gratuitous since anybody could come in through the windows. They walked back to the jeep, Beth edgy and bruised after arguing with the receptionist.

"I'm going to get a basin and a thermos of hot water to wash with, and then eat lunch and see the fort," Beth said.

Marco nodded.

Having a conversation with him was like talking to a mute. She longed for someone who chatted, who was voluble and offered details and information. Spiritual people _were_ dull. He didn't deserve even her worst efforts at seduction. Comparisons were odious and unavoidable: Paul could set a brisk conversational pace, and she imagined the jokes he would be making, the way he could make her laugh even when she was ill-tempered.

Back in the Pamir Hotel courtyard, Jean reappeared,

her cheeks flushed. "Look, Beth, I got these great plastic shoes and this bedspread."

"Nice," Beth said, pretending to be impressed with the standard-issue, cheap, Chinese merchandise.

"What appalling accommodations have you two found for us tonight?" Wayne asked, but he looked suspiciously pleased at the prospect.

"For this evening, we have two attractive rooms with a view for a paltry seven kuai each. Let's go, Gao," she said.

As they were getting in the jeep, Jean whispered, "The men in this town are quite good-looking, don't you think?"

Tashkurgan was a rough town, and Jean was interested in flirtations. Where was her sense?

Wayne and Jean stood in the doorway to their room, speechless. Beth had taken a broom from the Pamir Hotel and began sweeping the room she was going to share with Marco. They flipped the mattresses against the wall, and Marco swept the planks that formed the bed frames. The room was icy and grim, with dust thick in the air. Beth took the broom next door, but Jean was staring despondently out the window and hardly noticed. The jeep was parked in the courtyard; both Gao and Wayne had disappeared.

Back in their room, Marco was unrolling his sleeping pad and bag on one of the plank beds. Beth lay on her back, her knees bent, pressing her lower back flat against the board. Here, on their third night of sleeping beside each other, there was a kind of weary familiarity that usually came as a result of being with someone for years. Maybe seduction was more about her ego—a giant inflatable doll that she was obliged to carry everywhere—than about desire. She wanted to laugh at the image she had of herself, finessing a seduction while holding a puffed-up, overly pink, stiff-legged mannequin in her arms.

"I'll meet you in the courtyard of the Pamir Hotel in twenty minutes," she said. After Marco left, she first swallowed some pills, then poured water from the thermos into the wash basin, and with a cloth and a bit of soap, washed her face thoroughly, took off her clothes, and quickly rinsed. The water felt deliciously hot for less than a minute, and then it turned icy against her skin. There was far too little of it. She put on her last clean shirt, which nevertheless had several oily stains on it from noodle soup she'd eaten in Lanzhou, unbraided her hair, worked a wet comb through it, and rebraided it into a tight, thick rope. She looked at pieces of herself in her pocket mirror: a circle of her forehead, one of her eyes, a cheek. Poor quality.

She and Marco found the one open restaurant: a low, dark building dense with coal smoke. The place was filled with men all staring at Jean, who sat at a table, smiling weakly and eating a bowl of noodles. She'd brushed her hair into a wild halo of black curls.

They sat beside her. "Jean, these men are going to lose their minds if you don't cover your hair and get out of here. Where's Wayne?"

"I don't need a bodyguard."

Beth went to order. The kitchen was from the Middle Ages: walls furry with soot, woks as large as ponds steaming with prehistoric-sized yak bones, rivers of grease, coal fires glowing red and orange, a trough of slop overflowing with graying meat, fatty bits, rotting cabbage. Nothing tasty could issue from such a place. She ordered two plates of noodles, one with mutton and the other without. The noodles were gluey and thick, the mutton gristly, and the whole lot overly salted and slick with fat— nearly inedible. "I'm sorry. Obviously nobody knows how to cook here," she said.

"It doesn't matter." Marco smiled.

Predictably, Marco wasn't upset over something as trivial as sustenance.

"I'm going shopping," Jean said.

All the men watched her leave. "Shopping? In Tash-kurgan?" Beth said.

"'The Way is without picking or choosing; the waters are deep and the mountains steep,'" Marco said with a cryptic smile.

Oh, shut up with the nirvana nonsense. Anyway, she had work to do: she had to find them a ride over the border since she knew nobody else, including Mr. Enlightened beside her, seemed to have a self-preserving bone in their body.

Beth started talking to the men, making them laugh. "There's a guy here who will drive us to the border—it's a couple of hours—for twenty kuai each," she said to Marco. "We can leave early in the morning."

"Why are they laughing?"

"They asked about Jean and you." She smiled. "I told them Jean was married to the big, pale foreigner, and you were my son."

Marco coughed.

She felt suddenly satisfied. "And I told them you had long hair because American women find it sexy, and you like to have a lot of girlfriends."

He looked so uneasy it actually began to cheer her up. "So, tell me what happened with Emily."

"What?"

"Relax. I didn't read your journal; you said her name in your sleep."

Marco stared at her, guilty and guarded.

"Let's walk," she said.

They walked down Tashkurgan's single street to the fort.

A gust of wind cut up the street, swirling the dirt at their feet. They both turned their backs into it to zip their jackets. The sky was flat and thick with sooty clouds. From the fort ruins they had a bird's view of a man on camelback trotting through the valley along the Tashkurgan River. Piles of broken stones surrounded them, some of them resembling walls. "*Tashkurgan* means 'stone fortress' in Üighur, and these ruins are either six hundred or twenty-three hundred years old—I don't remember which. Ptolemy recommended Tashkurgan in his geography guide as a stop on the way to China, though what exactly he recommended is a little hard to imagine. Anyway, the famous peripatetic Buddhist monk Hsuan Tsang—you must know of him—came through in the seventh century, when it was the farthest frontier outpost of the Tang dynasty. And that's all I know." Beth paused; they were both watching the man riding the camel across the valley. The wind whistled through the piles of stones, and Beth wondered about others who had stood there, in the cold air pushed across this point, ears cocked for trouble. They wandered in silence down paths and through passages between crumbling walls; a dense silence that seemed intimate. Beth let herself relax into it, the restfulness of quiet. Maybe it was good for her to learn the virtues of silence. No, that was absurd; she adored entertainment, cleverness, wit, humor.

She sat on a crumpled wall in a wind-protected alcove. "Emily," she prompted.

"My girlfriend of ten years. Since high school. She got pregnant, and I didn't want to be a husband or father." Marco inhaled, swallowed, then turned sideways so he wouldn't have to look at Beth. "Not a surprising story." He smiled.

"You fled."

"I don't want an ordinary life."

"And the Buddhism?"

He shrugged.

"Penance," she said.

"Possibly."

"Is she having the child?"

"I don't know. I haven't heard from her; she doesn't want anything to do with me."

Beth couldn't look at him, didn't want to see heartache on his face.

"Just another irresponsible guy," he said.

Nobody was surprised by the irresponsibility of men. What could Beth say about her own failures of responsibility?

Before returning to their room, they stopped at the Pamir Hotel and filled their water bottles with boiling water. They were both tired, and Beth was looking forward to a cup of tea. They turned into their ill-kempt courtyard.

Jean and Gao stood beside the jeep, Gao's hand on Jean's hip, their faces just pulling apart from a kiss. Jean's hair looked like plucked turkey feathers, her face flushed pink as raw pork.

"Bad idea, Gao," Beth said. She could say anything since nobody else understood.

His laugh was harsh, like an animal being taken to slaughter. "It's her idea; she wants it."

"Think of yourself. What're you going to get out of this?" Beth said. *Beat up,* she thought.

"Money." Gao looked both afraid and triumphant. "She's paying me."

"Even worse."

"You slut." Wayne's voice echoed across the courtyard, against the brick walls. "We'll see how much you like fucking Chinamen. A lot of them. I've got your passport; you can stay here and fuck Chinamen for the rest of your life." He inhaled in a harsh rasp.

Jean lifted her head regally.

"Sleeping with an idiot who can't drive and spits all the time. Disgusting."

"Wayne: the great white fallen male. I'm not stupid. And don't think sex is so special with you." Her voice began to tremble.

"You have the bad taste to pick an ugly foreigner with rotten teeth." Wayne was jubilant and contemptuous.

"His teeth aren't rotten, and he's sweet."

Gao leaned against the jeep, bending his head and hovering around a cigarette, trying to get it lit.

Jean fluffed her hair, tucked in her blouse, and adjusted her coat. "You're a jerk," she said, almost to herself. "I'm sick of your insults and of you assuming I'm stupid; I know what you do."

She turned to Marco and Beth as to a jury. "When we travel, he leaves our room in the middle of the night. I used to be a sound sleeper. He wanted to go to Thailand, because there are a lot of whores there. Well." She paused and there was only the sound of the wind. Even Wayne waited for her to finish. "I can buy sex too."

Wayne turned to Gao. "Fool, you slept with a woman whose man is twice your size. Pathetic sod." Then he lunged at Gao, pinned him to the ground, and began pummeling him. Gao twisted and kicked, trying to shield his face, occasionally grunting.

"Wayne. Stop," Beth said.

Jean stood still, entranced by the spectacle of the two men grappling.

Marco strode forward and stepped hard on the arch of

Wayne's foot. He flipped like a fish, then rolled free, and turned to Marco.

"It's enough," Marco said. Wayne looked at Gao, groaning into the dirt.

Wayne dusted off his jeans. "Okay." He nodded, then began to walk away. There was a moment of almost reverential quiet.

Gao yanked a knife from the back of his pants and jumped at Wayne. Wayne flinched and twisted, but the knife caught his jacket sleeve, spilling feathers.

"Fucking wanker."

Gao bent low, dove for Wayne's legs, leaving him standing with rips in his jacket and his pants. "The fucker got me," Wayne said, dabbing a dot of blood from his leg. He seemed peaceful, almost as if he were enjoying himself.

Gao tucked his knife back into his pants. He, too, looked refreshed, even happy.

"Now what?" Beth asked him.

"I need a drink," Gao said. "Pay me the rest of the money."

"Right. Two hundred kuai." She counted out the notes, deciding it was easier to collect everyone's share later. Gao recounted the bills, smiling through the dirt smeared across his face. "I'll find passengers for the return. It's been a good trip," he said, and spat into the dirt, as if to seal the ending.

Wayne and Jean walked to their room as if nothing had happened.

In their own room, Marco set out a couple of candles and propped the mattresses against the shattered windows, providing privacy and slightly hindering the flow of cold air. Night came abruptly with a cold gloom. Beth shut the door and leaned her back against it. She could easily recall her own marriages, each of those break-ups, the itchy feeling of needing to move on, or the way her chest opened into a depthless hole of loss. Guilt, pressure, stress. Leaning against the door of this dirty, cold room, a sense of freedom filled her like air into a balloon, ready to float away; she was unattached, not married to anyone. She had nothing to mess up, no one to be unfaithful to, no one to hurt, no one to hurt her. Not for her, the toil of human intimacy. Marco blew out one of the candles, and lemony moonlight blunted the room's ugliness. He sat on her plank bed. "I don't know if I can really be celibate."

That sounded realistic. He took her hand.

"Are you hitting on me?" she said.

"I think so. It's been a while since I've done this." He stroked her cheek, put one hand in the curve of her back; her secret place of pain, of aging.

She hesitated. She liked him better for his honesty. She preferred sex combined with love, but sex without love was also fine; it was how she was. Still, she couldn't rouse desire. She felt bereft and elated, as if she'd won a prize that meant she'd have to give up everything familiar to her.

She kissed his cheek. "No." She didn't understand why, exactly. A belated, misplaced, uninvited loyalty to Paul? The mean, just pleasure of saying no to someone who seemed to always get what he wanted? The inexplicable, unfamiliar joys of restraint? A long overdue bow to reality?

Marco nodded, his face still, expressionless.

She got into her sleeping bag, feeling self-contained and pristine, the tidy virtue of being alone.

IV.

Gao walked carefully into the courtyard where Beth, Marco, and Jean were waiting for the new jeep and driver.

His head throbbed so hard he couldn't believe he was standing upright. He'd spent the night drinking in a stinking, ugly hole of a bar. At some point, Wayne walked in, and they had greeted each other like old friends. Wayne. Now they had things in common. Gao faced his jeep, too early, too hungover; he inhaled slowly, delicately. He didn't want to upset the fine balance of his system, which felt like the shivering filament inside a lightbulb on the verge of going out. Wayne would arrive soon, also hungover, and he actually knew something about engines.

"Have you eaten?" Beth asked Gao in a teasing tone; it was the usual morning greeting in China.

Gao paled at the thought of food. "Have eaten."

"Did you find passengers for the return?"

"Yes, one." He tried not to look at Jean, but he noticed that she'd chopped her hair off and wore it tied down by a piece of Chinese bedspread. A strange girl, but those breasts. He concentrated on extracting the keys from his pocket. Western women were different, but he wasn't sure how exactly. He couldn't figure it out in this state of mind anyway. Something for him to consider.

Wayne appeared, still wearing his slashed jeans with small, dark patches of dried blood. He put his head immediately beneath the jeep's hood. Wayne and Gao worked on the jeep, communicating with gestures and grunts. While the engine was idling, Wayne retrieved his pack and threw it in the jeep. The others stood quietly watching.

He took one of Gao's cigarettes and put his hand up to stroke his beard, but it was gone; it had been hacked off. "Gotta light? This wanker has cigarettes but no matches." He shook his head in disgust at Gao.

Beth pulled out her box of matches, struck one, and held it to Wayne's cigarette. "Aren't you coming with us?" she asked.

He shook his head.

"What are your plans, then?"

He inhaled so that his chest puffed up. "Stay here."

"Nice," she said. "Good food, lovely people, fabulous views, ideal weather."

Wayne nodded. "Fucking right."

"Are you sure this is going to be okay for you?" Beth asked Gao.

"No problem. We're friends."

"Did you cut his beard off?"

"The wife did."

Beth raised her eyebrows. "I didn't think she had it in her."

"No damage—just hair," Gao said.

Beth fiddled with her box of Double Happiness matches; the characters for "Double Happiness" were used at weddings, meant to bring good luck. She picked at the thin, red paper label, peeling away the golden characters and dropping bits of paper, curled like thin pieces of skin, until the box was only flimsy, gray cardboard.

"Take care of yourself, Gao." She had an urge to hug him, but she thought that might embarrass him. Instead, she handed him the denuded box of matches. "Keep these."

Beth looked over at Jean, who shrugged and giggled. But as Jean watched Wayne slam the hood and climb into the passenger seat, her forehead twitched and her eyes watered. "Got your passport?" Beth asked.

"Yeah. He kept the playing cards, I've got the camera." Then she tilted her head at Marco and said, "Are you going all the way to India?"

Marco nodded without speaking. For the first time, he looked noticeably disheveled, his hair greasy and uncombed, his clothing haphazard. His calm had finally sprung a leak. Beth felt no satisfaction. She swallowed some pills.

"You take pills often; what for?" Marco asked. How refreshingly blunt.

"I've got a bad back, and this trip has been hell on it."
It didn't make her sound old.

The next jeep pulled into the courtyard with two silent
Üighur men in the front. Jean coyly suggested that Marco
sit in the middle, and he did, ignoring the implications of
her tone. The road arced up the plateau out of Tashkurgan,
a long, graceful sweep of undisturbed snow. Yaks stood
in the distance, and the air was as thin as the blade edge
of a knife. Jean rolled down her window and tossed out
handfuls of Wayne's hair. Clumps of curly, strawberry-
blond hair blew apart in the wind, some of it fluffy and
light, some of it beard-coarse.

They traveled in a minivan down from the top of the
Khunjerab Pass, where they had passed through Chinese customs and immigration, to the town of Sust, where
Pakistan had its customs and immigration station. The
road was new, slick and black. The Pakistani driver
took to it like a racetrack, accelerating as they hummed
downward into the Hunza Valley. The bottom of the
van was rusted away in places, and the road could be
seen, passing below their feet in a blur. Jean laughed.
Beth gripped the seat back in front of her and wondered, if she were to die, what her final thoughts would
be. Of course she would dwell on her failures, which
clanged with the piercing clarity of church bells, while
her successes held no resonance. But when signs appeared around the more dangerous corners—Smile, then
Relax—she did both. They stopped at a military checkpoint, and a handsome, dark-eyed soldier stepped into
the van. "Welcome to Pakistan," he shouted. There was
a stunned silence until Jean asked if there was a loo
nearby. He flung his arms open and exclaimed, "You
may shit anywhere in Pakistan!"

Sust, Pakistan
Darling Paul,
I'm in Pakistan; different country, different life. I've got my own room, though no electricity or hot water. Still, the floors are swept, there's a kerosene lantern, and a single bed, which is some kind of message about myself; I've slept in nothing but single beds for months. Pakistan is immediately, obviously not China. First off, the men are gorgeous, nearly every one of them. Tall, dark, and handsome, stinking of sexuality. There's something unappealing about the whole thing: overkill. There's no subtlety here, no challenge, none of that irresistible tension. With hardly a smile, or a flash of my feathers, I could sleep with the entire town. All the fun is gone. I'm writing this in a teahouse with the waiter staring at me. No, that's not accurate—he's leering. He's practically drooling at the sight of a woman's face; a kind of stunned lechery. He can't believe his good luck. If I lifted my shirt, he'd faint. It makes me want to laugh. Maybe I can finally loosen my grip on desire, begin to appreciate monogamy and fidelity.

Yours, Beth

Now she had no one to be faithful to. She ripped up the sheet of paper, walked into the kitchen, and dropped the bits of letter into the orange glow of the coals. Three men planted on squat stools never took their eyes from her. Outside, jagged, gray peaks surrounded the town, the road deserted, the air quiet. She looked at the slab of dirty glacier slathered down one slope, wondering if it were possible to witness a glacier's movement, watch its stealthy slip.

KATHLEEN LEE has traveled extensively for two decades in Asia, South America, and the Middle East. She has written for *Condé Nast Traveler* magazine, and her work appears in *Best American Travel Writing 2001*. This is her first collection of stories. She lives in Pittsburgh.